The Burden

Nancy Rue

PUBLISHING
Colorado Springs, Colorado

THE BURDEN
Copyright © 1997 by Nancy N. Rue
All rights reserved. International copyright secured.

Library of Congress Cataloging-in-Publication Data
Rue, Nancy N.
    The burden / Nancy Rue.
       p.   cm. — (The Christian heritage series ; bk. 9)
    Summary: As the fighting between Patriots and Loyalists moves closer
to Williamsburg, eleven-year-old Thomas Hutchinson finds himself
burdened by all kinds of secrets involving the people closest to him.
    ISBN 1-56179-517-8
    1. Williamsburg (Va.)—History—Revolution, 1775–1783—Juvenile
fiction. [1. United States—History—Revolution, 1775–1783—
Fiction.   2. Williamsburg (Va.)—Fiction.   3. Christian life—
Fiction.]   I. Title.   II. Series: Rue, Nancy N.   Christian heritage
series ; bk. 9.
PZ7.R88515Bu   1997   96-44973
                                                      CIP
                                                       AC

Published by Focus on the Family Publishing,
Colorado Springs, Colorado 80995
Distributed in the U.S.A. and Canada by Word Books, Dallas, Texas.

No part of this publication may be reproduced, stored in a retrieval system, or
transmitted in any form or by any means—electronic, mechanical, photocopy,
recording, or otherwise—without prior permission of the publisher.

The author is represented by the literary agency of Alive Communications,
1465 Kelly Johnson Blvd., Suite 320, Colorado Springs, CO 80920.

This is a work of fiction, and any resemblance between the characters in this book and
real persons is coincidental.

Focus on the Family books are available at special quantity discounts when pur-
chased in bulk by corporations, organizations, churches, or groups. Special imprints,
messages, or excerpts can be produced to meet your needs. For more information,
write: Special Sales, Focus on the Family Publishing, 8605 Explorer Dr., Colorado
Springs, CO 80920; or call (719) 531-3400 and ask for the Special Sales Department.

Editor: Keith Wall
Cover Design: Bradley Lind
Cover Illustration: Cheri Bladholm

Printed in the United States of America

97 98 99 00/10 9 8 7 6 5 4 3 2 1

For Jacquie Reinhartsen,
who bears her cross with dignity and love.

A Map of
Williamsburg
1780–81

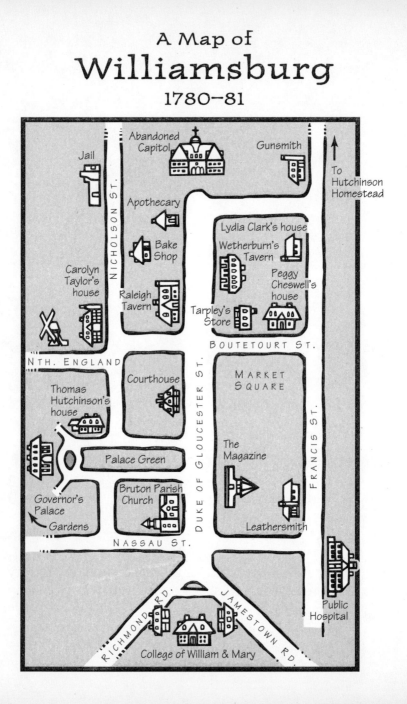

Jail

Abandoned Capitol

Gunsmith

To Hutchinson Homestead

NICHOLSON ST.

Apothecary

Lydia Clark's house

Bake Shop

Wetherburn's Tavern

Carolyn Taylor's house

Raleigh Tavern

Peggy Cheswell's house

Tarpley's Store

BOUTETOURT ST.

NTH. ENGLAND

Courthouse

MARKET SQUARE

Thomas Hutchinson's house

DUKE OF GLOUCESTER ST.

FRANCIS ST.

Palace Green

The Magazine

Governor's Palace Gardens

Bruton Parish Church

Leathersmith

NASSAU ST.

Public Hospital

RICHMOND RD.

JAMESTOWN RD.

College of William & Mary

Chapter One

"Tom Hutchinson, stop your pouting!" said
Caroline Taylor.

Although she was a head shorter and had
arms like willow branches, she gave Thomas a poke in the
ribs as she trotted beside him to keep up.

"I'm not pouting," Thomas growled at her. He could see
his own dark eyebrows, he was scowling so hard.

In front of them, lanky Malcolm Donaldson turned to
deliver one of his square smiles. "Then why would your lip
be stickin' out so far that Caroline could near sit on it?"

Thomas sucked in his lower lip and frowned at them
both.

Caroline's face broke into a thousand dimples. "You try
to be so tough, Thomas," she said. "But you don't scare anyone anymore."

"Come on, then, lad," Malcolm said as he shortened his

1

long strides to walk beside them. Though four years older than Thomas, Malcolm was the same height and much skinnier. Thomas's hard muscles made it difficult for some people to believe he was only 11. It was a Hutchinson trait he would have been proud of if—

"Watch out!" Caroline cried.

But it was too late. Thomas hadn't seen the loose stone that jutted out of the sidewalk on Nassau Street and had caught the toe of his silver-buckled shoe. He was sprawled face first on the walk before Malcolm could even grab for him.

"Whoa there, lad!" Malcolm said, extending his hand.

But Thomas pushed it away and scrambled to his feet. Caroline didn't even try to hide her smile—the one that exposed her big, white, shiny teeth.

"Oaf," she said, brown eyes dancing a jig.

In spite of himself, Thomas could almost feel his own deep-set blue eyes starting to twinkle.

"You've got him, lassie!" Malcolm said. When Malcolm was delighted, his small, black eyes seemed to send out sparks, and they were doing it now. The Scottish servant boy cuffed Thomas's dark, wiry curls. "He's laughin' now, eh?"

"I'm not!"

Caroline put her hands pertly on the slender waist of her rust-colored dress. The wide elbow ruffles tossed about like leaves in the brisk autumn breeze. "Well, if you aren't pouting and you aren't laughing," she said, "what *are* you doing?"

Thomas looked around in his mind for a word that

Alexander—Caroline's older brother and his teacher— might be proud of. "I'm . . . I'm smoldering," he said finally.

Malcolm let out a slow, impressed whistle. Caroline's nearly invisible sandy eyebrows knitted together. She brushed back a stray wisp of blond hair that had crept out from under her cap as she frowned at him.

"Stop showing off," she said. "What does that mean— *smoldering?*"

"I'm trying to hold back the heat of my anger," Thomas said.

"That's news for the *Virginia Gazette,* then, lad," Malcolm said, still grinning. "And good news at that. I've been on the punchin' end of your anger!"

Caroline stopped dead at the corner of Francis and Nassau Streets and planted her hands on her tiny waist once more. "Have you two been fighting again? I thought that was all over."

"No!" Thomas cried.

Malcolm winked. "He knows better."

Thomas started to protest, but Caroline cut in quickly.

"What are you angry about, Tom?" she asked.

Thomas kicked miserably at the stone walkway and folded his arms across his big-for-an-11-year-old chest. He could feel the coarse, homespun Virginia cloth of his full sleeves scratching his arms. There was a time when only smooth silk and soft linen would have touched his skin. With the War for Independence going on, those things were hard to come by in 1780. But that wasn't the part of the war and its changing times that was making him "smolder."

Malcolm propped his foot up on the lower crossbar of a fence and waited for an answer. He wore breeches of faded red stripes made from even coarser material, but unlike Thomas, he'd never been dressed better before coming to Williamsburg, Virginia, from Scotland last summer as the Hutchinsons' indentured servant. Although his shoes tied rather than buckled, and he almost always wore a leather apron, he seemed to Thomas to be thankful for everything Thomas's father, John Hutchinson, provided for him.

"Well?" Malcolm said. "Let's have it, then, shall we?"

Thomas shrugged. Caroline gave him another poke, and he cracked open.

"I hate it that they've taken over the old abandoned Governor's Palace for a hospital!" he blurted out.

"Come now, laddie," Malcolm said, his dark face suddenly serious. "It's for the Patriot cause!"

"I know," Thomas said sullenly. "Papa says the war is moving closer and they're going to need a place to take care of the wounded soldiers."

"There will be patients there soon," said Malcolm. "There's been some fightin' in North Carolina."

Thomas darted a glance at Caroline. She had picked up a crimson maple leaf that had drifted to the ground and was examining its veins as if he and Malcolm were speaking a foreign language and there was no point in trying to listen. But Thomas knew she heard every word, and a pang of guilt flashed through him.

Usually he didn't talk about the war in front of her. Caroline's father—gentle, serious Robert Taylor, owner of the town mill—was a Loyalist. He didn't believe that the Americans should be fighting for independence from England. He never made trouble, and he didn't try to help the British soldiers, and for that Thomas's Patriot father was grateful. John Hutchinson's job was to protect the Loyalists in Williamsburg from being harmed by angry Patriots like Xavier Wormeley, the magistrate who was always trying to run the Taylors out of town—or worse.

Still, sometimes it was hard being Caroline's best friend when their fathers' beliefs were so different. If she weren't the most fun person he'd ever known—even though she *was* a girl—it would have been impossible.

"The Palace was such a good place for our games," Thomas said. "Especially in the gardens."

"I know," Caroline said. "I miss the Chinese Bridge most."

"From what you've told me," Malcolm said, "we were only able to play there because Governor Thomas Jefferson abandoned it to move to Richmond."

Thomas looked back at sleepy little Williamsburg, quiet even for early evening. "And took most of the town with him, Papa says. It used to be the center of the Virginia colony."

"Well, thank goodness it isn't no more," said Malcolm, pulling his foot from the fence. "Or there wouldn't be any place for our Fearsome Trio."

Thomas began to chew on the inside of his mouth, as he always did when he was trying to figure things out, if he weren't biting his fingernails instead. The Fearsome Trio was the name he, Malcolm, and Caroline had given themselves last summer. He was Thomas the Tireless, and there was Caroline the Courageous and Malcolm the Mighty. Together, behind the empty Governor's Palace in the over-grown gardens, they had created a world of their own, a world of adventure, a world where it didn't matter that Caroline was a girl or that Malcolm was a servant or that Thomas was a "clumsy oaf." And because they were a team, they'd been able to help Williamsburg and even the war last summer. But now it looked as if there was nowhere for them to go anymore.

"There isn't any place," Thomas said to them as he followed Malcolm across Francis Street with Caroline behind him.

Malcolm wiggled his bushy black eyebrows. "Ah, but there is, lad."

Caroline scooted out from behind Thomas and squeezed her face into a doubtful expression. "Where?"

In answer, Malcolm pointed to a two-story brick building that brooded over Francis Street from under a roof made of curled-up cypress shingles. The cupola on top was peeling with paint that had blistered in the sun several summers ago, and the copper weather vane spun in a crazy, lopsided fashion in the blustery wind.

"Are you talking about *that* place?" Caroline asked.

"For us to play in?" Thomas said.

Malcolm nodded proudly. "I discovered it yesterday. It's perfect."

"No!"

Thomas wasn't sure whether he or Caroline shouted it the loudest. Caroline plastered her hands over her mouth, and Thomas felt his eyes bulging from his head.

"What's the matter with it?" Malcolm bristled. "It looks like it hasn't been used in years. Probably somethin' belonging to the British before they all escaped from here five years ago."

"It *is* being used!" Caroline said.

"And not by the British!" Thomas said.

"Who would allow a buildin' to fall to ruin like that if they were still usin' it?" Malcolm asked. He let one side of his mouth go up. "I even looked in some of the windows, and the rooms are practically empty."

Caroline clutched at the lace on her neckline. "You didn't!"

"What is ailin' the two of you?" Malcolm said. "I never took you for cowards. Not after all we've been through."

"When you peeked in the windows, didn't you notice the bars on them?" Thomas said.

Malcolm nodded. "So?"

"They're there to keep the patients inside!"

"What patients?"

"The crazy ones!" Caroline cried.

Malcolm stared at her.

"It's the Public Hospital for Persons of Insane and Disordered Minds." Thomas repeated it just the way his oldest brother, Clayton, had corrected him when Thomas had first spoken of "crazy people."

"They are just people who are so unhappy that they've lost their ability to reason like the rest of us," Clayton had told him sternly. Clayton had studied to be a minister and said everything as if it were a sermon. He'd explained in his preacher voice that the hospital was the only one of its kind in America devoted entirely to helping people who couldn't help themselves find their lost senses.

Thomas had never believed Clayton as readily as he did his middle brother, Sam, but he always hurried when he had to walk by the building anyway. He'd heard talk that strange things went on in there. No one ever said what those things were, but Thomas's own imagination made him shiver.

Malcolm was gazing at the hospital. "They still use it, you say?"

"Not very much anymore, my father told me," Caroline answered. "Most of the doctors who take care of the patients have gone away to the war." She tugged at Malcolm's sleeve. "Please, can we go?"

"What are you afraid of?" Malcolm said. "There're bars on the windows."

"But sometimes they let the people out to exercise in the yard," she said. "I just don't want to see . . . a madman."

Malcolm looked as if he did, but to Thomas's relief, he sighed and shrugged. "All right, then. I'll just have to keep lookin' for a place to have our adventures. I thought I'd found it sure."

"Perhaps the old Capitol Building," Thomas said, edging away from the hospital.

Malcolm grunted. "Too close to the Duke of Gloucester Street. If there is any activity in Williamsburg, it's usually there."

"Let's go look anyway," Caroline said, now yanking on his arm in earnest.

Malcolm delivered a rectangular grin and let her pull him along. "I never knew you to be afraid of anything, lassie," he said.

As the Fearsome Trio—two-thirds of which had now admitted they were afraid of the Public Hospital for Persons of Insane and Disordered Minds—headed down Francis Street and left it behind, Thomas's spirits lifted a little. It was a brisk autumn afternoon, and the trees were a blur of scarlets, flames, and violets against a sky so deep-blue it made Thomas's eyes ache. A flock of geese honked overhead as they winged their way south, and the Bruton Parish Church bell pealed the approach of Evensong.

For a few laughing, leaf-rustling minutes, Thomas almost forgot that there was even a war going on to the south of them . . . until from a yard on the corner of Francis and Waller Streets, a shot cracked through the air, and a woman screamed.

"What was that?" Caroline cried.

"It sounded like a gun!" Thomas looked wildly at Malcolm. "Didn't it to you?"

But Malcolm didn't answer. He raced toward the yard with the rest of the Fearsome Trio at his heels.

✝ ⚜ ✝

Chapter Two

homas's heart hammered against the inside of his chest as he tore after Malcolm toward the narrow yellow house. Because he delivered medicine for Francis Pickering, the apothecary, Thomas knew it was where Peggy Cheswell lived.

Has she been shot? Thomas thought frantically as they followed her screams to the outbuildings behind her house. *Who would shoot an old widow?*

It didn't occur to him to think that if someone *had* shot her, the shooter would probably still be standing there with a smoking gun that he could turn on the Fearsome Trio. Evidently, it did occur to Malcolm, because he stopped outside the stable and whispered, "She's in there. Stay here."

As the oldest—and the one with the most experience—Malcolm was always protective of Caroline and Thomas.

But as he tiptoed toward the stable, they were right in his wake. It was hard for any one of them to do anything without the other two these days.

Still, Thomas's heart continued to thunder in his ears, and the Widow Cheswell continued to scream. When Malcolm pushed open the door to the darkened stable, her words bled through the racket she was making.

"Oh, no!" she was shrieking. "I thought you were a thief! I didn't mean to! I didn't mean to!"

With that, Malcolm flung open the door wide, and the dwindling autumn light revealed Peggy Cheswell in its path. Thomas and Caroline crowded in behind Malcolm.

"Glory be!" Malcolm cried.

At once, Thomas saw it, too. There in the corner, hunched down in the straw, was a little girl.

Dressed in a brick-colored gown that was miles too big for her, she was tinier than Caroline, and she stared at them through a thick fringe of shaggy black hair. But even at that, Thomas could see she had green eyes the size of saucers that were right now swimming in terror.

Malcolm, however, saw something else. He took the stable in two strides and bent over the crumpled figure. "She's bleedin' bad!"

"I didn't mean to!" the Widow Cheswell cried again. "With all the horse thievin' that went on last summer, I thought she was some Loyalist thief come to take my only horse!"

Only then did Thomas see the pistol in her hand. She looked as if she didn't know how it had gotten there or what to do with it now that it had. Uncurling her fingers, she dropped it into the straw.

"You shot her?" Malcolm said. His eyes were boring into the widow like bullets themselves.

"It's so dark—"

"She needs the doctor!" Malcolm cried.

"I'll get Nicholas Quincy!" Caroline said. Even in the dark of the stable, Thomas could see that her face was pasty pale. He was sure his own looked the same.

"Do you know where he is, Tom?" she called.

"He was going to Wetherburn's for supper when I left Francis's shop."

"Go!" Malcolm said. "And hurry!"

Caroline flew from the stable, and Thomas bolted after her, calling, "Tell Dr. Quincy to come straight here! I'll bring what he needs from the apothecary shop!"

So they both dashed toward the Duke of Gloucester Street, which ran through the center of Williamsburg. On the way, the thoughts whirled in Thomas's head. *He'll need his surgical instruments to get the bullet out. And salt petre to put in the wound. And probably some salt of ammonia to keep it from rotting.*

As he dodged the puddles on the muddy main street, Thomas looked nervously at the few shops that were still in business. Most of their owners had locked up for the day and left the shop windows candleless and dark. If Francis weren't there, they would lose precious time. Thomas had helped Nicholas with enough wounds to know that it was important to hurry.

Almost automatically, he began to talk to God. He'd started praying last spring when he'd come to Williamsburg and learned that God was real. *Please let me get there in time,* he prayed.

Half a myrtle-wax candle was still guttering its way down in the front window of the apothecary shop. Thomas nearly blew it out as he burst through the front door.

Old Francis squinted up from his vials and jars. "Slow down there, boy!" he said in his wheezy voice.

"I can't!" Thomas huffed out. "A girl's been shot, over at the Widow Cheswell's!"

Francis's beady old eyes sprang open, and the spectacles tottered off his nose. He was already headed for the salt petre canister.

"Have you called for Nicholas?" he said as he filled a cloth bag.

"Caroline went for him."

"Then it's sure he'll get there. She's a good, dependable girl."

As much as he hated Loyalists, old Francis had only good things to say about the Taylors. They had helped save his life once, and he had never forgotten it. But then, Thomas knew, Francis Pickering never forgot anything. He might be ancient and half-blind, but his mind was sharp. Nicholas said the old man was the finest apothecary he'd ever worked with. That was probably why the two were partners now in Williamsburg. As Francis's apprentice, Thomas liked to think of himself as part of that team.

"Will you be taking the wounded girl home?" Francis

asked as he handed the bundle of medicines to Thomas. "Or shall I get the room ready here?"

Thomas took the bundle, picked up the long wooden box of surgical instruments, and headed for the door. "I don't even know who she is," he said over his shoulder. "I never saw her before."

Francis looked sharply at him over his spectacles. A stranger in Williamsburg was a rare thing, especially a child alone.

What was she doing in the Widow Cheswell's stable all by herself? Thomas wondered as he tore back to the stable on Francis Street. *Stealing horses? Not a prayer of it!*

Not only was the little girl delicate-looking enough to be blown away by one gust of Virginia's autumn wind, but she looked too frightened to steal so much as a sewing needle. Thomas was sure he'd never seen such terror in a person's eyes.

He arrived on the heels of Caroline and Dr. Nicholas Quincy, whose pearl-gray coat was flying out behind him as he entered the stable. Tall, thin, pale, and frail, Nicholas usually looked like a shy, backward shopkeeper. But when he was intent on saving someone's life, he looked as he did now—strong, determined, and surrounded by God's light.

"Did you bring—?" he began.

"Everything, sir," Thomas said.

He would have rattled off a list, but the sight of the little girl in the straw stopped him cold. He looked at Caroline with his mouth open. She looked back the same way.

The tiny person who minutes before had looked as if she

would tremble right out of their sight was stretched out on the straw with a blanket over her. Malcolm was stooped beside her, holding both of her elfin hands in his, and she was gazing up at him—smiling.

Smiling? Thomas thought. He blinked. Her smile revealed a mouth crowded full of crooked teeth and produced a miniature dimple in each cheek.

"Hello, my dear," Nicholas said in his soft voice. "I see you're in good hands." He examined her for a moment, then said, "Thank the Lord you only got hit in the foot."

Meanwhile, the little girl looked up at Malcolm with adoring eyes. If Thomas hadn't been so dumbfounded, he was sure he would have squirmed. He liked Caroline and all that, but touching a girl and having her look at him like that was something else again.

"Thomas," Nicholas said in as sharp a voice as he ever used.

Thomas leaped to his side with the medicines and instruments, and their work began.

Through it all—removing the bullet from her foot, cleaning the wound, packing the hole—Nicholas prayed soundlessly as he always did when he was doctoring, and the little girl never uttered a whimper. Caroline, on the other hand, watched from behind the Widow Cheswell's apron and cringed. The only thing the wounded child insisted on was clutching Malcolm's hand. But she never said a word.

"Perhaps you can get her to talk to us, Malcolm," the doctor said.

"I don't think I'd be wantin' to talk either, sir," Malcolm

said. He glared at Mistress Cheswell. "She's only just been shot, after all."

"I didn't mean to!" the widow whined.

Caroline patted her arm.

"Still and all, I'd like to take her home and finish up there, where she can lie in a clean bed, and I can give her mother instructions on how to care for her. Can't you please at least get her to tell us where she lives?"

Malcolm tried, though not very hard as far as Thomas was concerned.

He sure has taken to protecting this girl, Thomas thought. *And she's sure taken to hanging on him.*

"Well, then," said Nicholas, "I suppose we shall have to take her to the apothecary to stitch her up. Perhaps someone will search for her parents in the meantime." He looked around the stable as if he didn't know exactly who he had in mind.

Caroline let go of the widow and saluted smartly. She'd watched the soldiers drill on the Palace Green all summer. "At your service, sir!" she said.

Nicholas looked at Malcolm, but the little girl squeezed his hand so hard that Thomas could see her knuckles turning white.

"Perhaps Malcolm should assist me and you should go and help Caroline search," Nicholas said to Thomas. "I doubt we'll get this little one to let go of him anyway."

The Widow Cheswell gave a weak cough. "If you don't find anyone tonight," she said, wringing her hands together like two dishrags, "she can stay here. It's the very least I can do."

Malcolm sniffed, but Nicholas nodded graciously at the frightened old woman. "That would be very kind of you," the doctor said.

"Good-bye, girl," Caroline said to the small figure on the straw. "We'll find your mama and papa."

"As long as we don't know her name," Malcolm said, "why don't we think of one to call her? I don't imagine she likes being called *girl*."

"How about 'Georgianna'?" Caroline asked dreamily. "I love that name."

Thomas was about to comment that the name was bigger than the girl, when Malcolm said, "What about 'Patsy'?"

"Why Patsy?" asked Caroline.

Malcolm shrugged. "I don't know. I heard it was the name of one of Governor Thomas Jefferson's daughters. That makes it all right, eh?"

"All right," Caroline said with a sigh. "I'll save Georgianna for another time."

It was almost dark by now, and the windows of the houses danced with candle flickers as Thomas and Caroline made their way down the street.

"We might as well start with this one," Caroline said, pointing to a white clapboard house.

"No sense going there," Thomas said. "They moved away when they heard the war was coming to Virginia."

"What about here?" Caroline said, pointing to another house.

"The leathersmith's. I've taken cough troches to them. They have four boys, all in the army."

Caroline gazed at him in the gathering twilight. "Is there any house in this town you haven't been to, Tom?"

Thomas thought for a moment and then shook his head. "No," he answered. "I guess everyone needs medicine sometime."

Caroline chewed thoughtfully on a fingernail, a habit she'd picked up from Thomas. He started in on his, too.

"Then she must be a stranger in town," she said finally, "which means her parents are at one of the inns, or maybe visiting someone."

"Let's try an inn, then. The Raleigh first."

They were just about to pull open the heavy front door of the Raleigh Tavern when a voice called from the corner across the street.

"Caroline!" came the shout. "Where have you been?"

They both looked up to see Robert Taylor hurrying toward them, swinging a lantern that showed a tight face.

Caroline rushed up to him. "Papa, you won't believe what's happened!" she cried.

But the usually gentle mill owner didn't give her a chance to explain. He took his daughter almost roughly by the arm, and Thomas stepped back in surprise.

"I've been sick to death with worry, and so has your mother!" Robert said.

"But Papa—"

"I have enough on my mind without having to come looking for you in the dead of night!"

It's hardly the dead of night, Thomas wanted to say. But he choked the words back. Robert Taylor was half walking, half dragging a bewildered Caroline back across the street, and he didn't look as if he wanted to be argued with.

"Good night, Caroline," Thomas called out instead.

Caroline looked back at him helplessly and then disappeared into the shadows with her angry father. Thomas could only stand there staring in disbelief. Robert Taylor might as well have been as much a stranger as Patsy, shouting and being rough. He had never seen Caroline's father act that way.

✢ ✢ ✢

Chapter Three

𝕴t didn't look as if Caroline's father was going to be much help in finding Patsy's parents. But Thomas knew Papa would be. John Hutchinson was an important man in Williamsburg—what with being on the vestry of Bruton Parish Church and being responsible for protecting the rights of the Loyalists, besides owning his own plantation and shipyard in Yorktown. Even though Thomas's brother Clayton ran the Hutchinson Homestead while he was waiting to be ordained as a minister, the huge wheat plantation was still Papa's responsibility. Clayton walked with a limp and had a weak heart. Even though Nicholas was treating him with new medicine that was helping him, Clayton couldn't do everything Papa could.

As Thomas hurried through the damp chill toward their house on the Palace Green, Thomas knew his father would help with Patsy. There was a time he wouldn't have listened to Thomas, and with good reason. Thomas had been a bully with a bad temper. But since they'd come to Williamsburg, Thomas had changed. He was studying with Alexander and working hard for Francis and Nicholas. He knew God now, and he didn't throw temper tantrums anymore. He knew after last summer that he was close to winning Papa's respect and being as important in Papa's eyes as Sam and Clayton.

Candles and the light from the fireplace glowed softly through the Hutchinsons' dining room window as Thomas hurried up the brick steps and into the front hall. To his left, the partly open door let out the sounds of his family gathered in the butterscotch-colored room for supper.

"Have some pumpkin bread, John?" Mama was saying in the voice that always sounded like a song.

"Did Esther make it?" Papa said suspiciously in his deep voice—the one that always sounded like a command even when he was joking.

"No, sir," Mama chided him. "Betsy Taylor sent it over."

"Ah, that's a relief!" said still another voice, this one carrying a hint of adventure, as usual.

Thomas stopped with his hand on the doorknob. It was Sam, his 17-year-old brother, who lived around the corner at the College of William and Mary. He hadn't been home for a meal since the new school term had started. Before that, Sam at the table had usually meant an argument with Papa. Thomas wasn't sure what it meant now, after what had happened last summer.

But he hurried in. For all his hot-headedness, Sam was

still Thomas's favorite brother.

"Well, Thomas," Papa boomed from the head of the table. "It's about time you appeared."

Mama began to push bowls of potatoes and squash at him before he could even slide into his side chair across the table from Sam.

"Hello, little brother," Sam said.

Thomas studied him carefully. Sam's tiny blue eyes were still sparkling, and his curly blond hair didn't look as if he'd raked his hands through it. That meant he hadn't started badgering Papa—yet.

"What's the matter?" Sam said. "Have I grown an extra nose or something?"

"No!" Thomas said, so enthusiastically that he knocked over the salt dish and sent the tiny spoon tinkling against the bowl of boiled potatoes.

"Yes, you will want salt on those," Sam said, grinning. He turned to Papa as Thomas dished a helping of potatoes into his porringer. "Father, really, when are you going to bring in a decent cook? We all love Esther, but heaven knows she can ruin an apple pulling it from the tree!"

Papa's blue eyes, deep set like Thomas's, twinkled. "Esther's cooking is good for the character."

"Please don't let her hear you!" Mama whispered. Her big gray eyes glanced anxiously toward the door. "I wouldn't dream of hurting her feelings!"

Thomas smothered a grunt. *If Esther has feelings, it's news to me,* he thought. *She'd rather scold me than do anything else.*

The old servant and her husband, Otis, had been with the Hutchinsons since before Thomas's father was born. When they all lived on their plantation in Yorktown, the only thing she had to do was take care of the children. Since Papa had brought Thomas and his mother to live here in Williamsburg last spring, she had become their cook. Everyone had lost weight as a result . . . except Thomas. He dumped more salt on his potatoes and dug in.

"No wonder you're growing like you are," said Sam, whose own shoulders were wide and square like their father's. "You'll eat nearly anything."

"Not Esther's biscuits," Thomas said. "I chipped a tooth on one once."

"Thomas, you didn't!" Mama cried.

Papa laughed and patted her china-white hand.

Thomas cleared his throat. "I have news. Tonight, a girl was—"

"Wait, please, Thomas," Papa said, putting his palm forward. He turned to Sam. "I'm sure you want to know what I've heard of the war, so let us get that out of the way." Then looking at Thomas, he said, "You'll let your older brother go first, yes?"

For a moment, Thomas was stung. Papa was smiling at him. Sam was waiting patiently. But it was just that he'd thought—

"Thomas?" Papa said, his eyes curious.

"Yes, sir," Thomas said quickly.

Papa's eyes flickered to Sam.

"There is bad trouble in Carolina," he began. "The British

have turned brutal. It's said they have carried off everything from silver to slaves."

"Is it that new Redcoat general, Cornwallis?" Sam asked.

"No. It's a British officer by the name of Tarleton. His
men all wear green jackets and raid like ruthless dragoons."

Thomas wasn't sure what *dragoons* were, but Alexander
had taught him that "ruthless" meant "without any pity."
*Sort of the way Robert Taylor had treated Caroline this
evening,* he thought with a shiver.

"They're bedeviling the people and destroying their
property," Papa went on before Thomas could cut in. "And
what's worse, they seem to be headed toward Virginia."

Sam nodded grimly. "With all of Virginia's militia
already fighting out of the colony, that doesn't leave anyone
here for protection." He grunted. "Even Governor Jefferson
has run for cover. It boils my blood that Virginians have
been so helpless in this war. When our militia has marched
to a battle, it's been over before they got there."

Here it comes, Thomas thought miserably. *Sam's going
to say the army needs good men like him more than ever
now . . . and he's going to tell Papa he wants to quit school
and join Francis Marion in South Carolina . . . and Papa's
going to start yelling that he has to stay here and finish
his education . . . and Mama's going to start crying.*
Thomas poked at his potatoes and waited.

But Sam only continued with "Pass the pumpkin bread,
would you please, Mother?"

"I can't argue with you, Samuel," Papa said. "Our only
success in the South so far has been with Marion in the

swamps of Carolina." He chuckled. "The British don't know what hits them when those guerrillas rise up out of the marshes."

Thomas looked at Sam. Thomas expected him to say, "I want to go and fight with them, Father."

But Sam only chewed thoughtfully.

"I'm afraid I have other disturbing news," Papa said. He shook his gold-and-silver-haired head sadly. "General Washington has discovered that one of his favorite generals, Benedict Arnold, has turned traitor."

"Traitor!" Mama said, her black curls trembling from beneath her cap. "My goodness!"

"What's that mean?" Thomas asked.

"A traitor is someone who turns against the cause he has professed loyalty to and goes over to the other side, carrying all he knows with him."

"He's a spy, then?" Sam said.

"No. A spy sneaks about and pretends to remain on his own side. A traitor throws his disloyalty into the face of the people who have supported him."

"The scoundrel!" Sam said. "He could be telling the British everything he knows about the American fighting plan."

"They say he is a brigadier general in the British army now."

"The Lord help him if he ever shows up here," Sam said, his face red from his square jaw to the roots of his sandy hair.

Thomas started to chew on the inside of his mouth. *Now it's coming,* he thought. *Sam won't be able to hold back.*

"Let us hope the good Lord doesn't help Benedict Arnold," Papa said. "I have heard rumors that he will begin raiding up and down the James River any day now."

"The James River!"

Mama clasped her delicate hands over her mouth, but her eyes were wide with fear, and Thomas knew why. The James River was just a few miles away. He and Sam had been swimming in it together. And now the British were going to be on its shores—with their guns—and what was it Papa had said? "Bedeviling the people like ruthless dragoons"?

"General Washington will not leave us here at Arnold's mercy," Papa said to his wife, as if he were soothing a child. "My guess is that he will send that Frenchman Lafayette to resist the British. It's time he used the French. They've been in America for months, waiting to be of service to the Patriots."

"I think then you'll see the Virginians rally to the cause," Sam said. The fire was in his eyes, and once again Thomas sucked in his breath. But once again, Sam merely smeared butter on his pumpkin bread.

"I hope you're right, Samuel," Papa said. "It has been four years since the Declaration of Independence, and the British are still among us. Our government is so new, it barely knows how to run itself. Our army is starving and unpaid. There are companies where the soldiers have no tents, and some are drinking water from puddles. We've lost one army by capture at Charleston and another by sheer destruction in Camden. If something isn't done soon, I fear we've lost the war."

"Then let me go and help"—*that's what Sam is going to say now,* Thomas thought. He slanted a glance at his brother. Sam sat studying his tankard.

"I thought I'd done all I could for the cause of independence," Papa said. "I've donated much of my fortune to Washington's army. I've built warships at my docks in Yorktown. I've tried to keep the people of Williamsburg from giving up. . . ."

Papa sighed and looked around the table at his family. "So, it looks as if I must pray for God to tell me what else I must do to make certain that my sons will live in a free country. That is my cross to bear." Then he said, "What time is it, do you suppose?"

Sam pulled his watch from the pocket of his waistcoat, and Thomas couldn't help the wave of envy that washed over him. The gold timepiece, shaped like a globe, shone in the candlelight as it swung from its chain. Although he couldn't see them from across the table, Thomas knew the initials DH were engraved in the case. The watch had belonged to their grandfather, Daniel Hutchinson, and Papa had given it to Sam on his sixteenth birthday, just as on Clayton's sixteenth, he had given him the Bible that had belonged to their great-grandfather Josiah.

The snap of the watch case interrupted his thoughts.

"It's nearly eight o'clock," Sam said.

"Shall we gather in the parlor for evening prayer, then?" Papa said.

But before the family could push back their chairs, the door opened and wide-hipped Esther sailed in with Malcolm behind her. She carried a tray for clearing the table, and Malcolm's arms were loaded with wood to feed the fire. Esther nodded her gray head absently at everyone as she placed the dishes on the tray with her gnarled old hands. While she was at it, she gave Thomas a scolding frown and clicked her tongue. *Just in case I've done something I wasn't supposed to while she wasn't here,* he thought.

"We won't be needing a fire in here for the rest of the evening," Papa said to Malcolm. "But perhaps you could build one in the parlor. We were just going there."

Malcolm nodded politely and carried the armload of fire-wood across the hall.

"There is one of the best investments I've ever made," Papa said as he gazed at Malcolm. "That's a fine young man, and I know he has a good future ahead of him. Our country needs his sort."

"You're right, sir," Esther said, as if she had been solely responsible for bringing Malcolm to their home. "There's nothing I ask of the lad that he can't do—or won't do."

Once again, she deposited a frown on Thomas, who couldn't resist scowling back at her. But he ignored the angry prickles that started at the back of his neck. Esther still thought he was a bully and a brat. He wasn't going to do anything to prove her right.

Still, as he knelt in the parlor while Papa read the service of Evening Prayer from the *Book of Common Prayer,* Thomas's mind wandered uneasily back to the scene in the dining room. He wanted to pray, too, but he liked to wait until they got to the part where Papa said his own prayers. That's when God seemed close, as far as Thomas was concerned.

When I was a bully, none of them wanted to be around me, he thought now. *They swatted me aside like an annoying fly.*

Now I try to do what they expect, and I'm still ignored. Just when I thought I was as important to Papa as Clayton and Sam—and even Malcolm—I find out I'm not!

His neck stiffened angrily, but Thomas squeezed his eyes shut tight.

It won't do any good to be a bully again, he thought. *But what can I do?*

"Heavenly Father," Papa said. "You know the desires of our hearts. Please listen now, as we place them before you."

A thought flashed through Thomas's head. *Here's mine,* he said silently. *Please let me prove to them that I'm a "good investment," too.* Then just to be sure, he added, *Whatever it takes.*

He had no idea what that prayer was going to mean.

✢ ✦ ✢

Chapter Four

Thomas was grumpy as he sat in the dining room for lessons with Alexander the next morning, staring up at the delft blue china in the corner cabinet, but seeing only his jumbled dream from the night before.

In the dream, it had been Caroline who had been shot—by a man named Benedict Arnold who looked like Williamsburg's floppy-jowled magistrate, Xavier Wormeley. Thomas knew exactly what to do for her, but a whole line of people kept shoving him out of the way—Papa, Sam, Clayton, Malcolm, even Esther. Especially Esther. She had thrown him out into the street where he'd had to drink water out of a puddle. That's where he was when a herd of dragons in green jackets had run over him trying to get to the silverware.

"Have you been eating Esther's hoe cakes again?"

Alexander Taylor asked him. "You look positively ill."

Thomas didn't answer but said instead, "What is a 'dragoon'?"

As usual, Alexander didn't roll his eyes as if Thomas had asked a silly question, the way most teachers did. He just slanted his slender frame back in the side chair and laced his fingers on his red vest. Thomas noticed that it was frayed around the buttons. Like Thomas, who had on a vest and breeches that were straining at the seams, Alexander was wearing last year's clothes because no one could get cloth from England anymore. Even Mama, who had seldom done more than serve tea on the plantation, was sewing new lace on old velvet gowns these days and cheerfully saying it was her way of fighting the war.

"A dragoon," Alexander said, "is a soldier who carries a pistol and is very good at shooting it from the back of a horse."

Thomas's mood grew even darker.

"Why?" Alexander said, brown eyes crackling merrily. "Have you see one?"

"No," Thomas snapped. "But I think we're about to!"

"Ah." Alexander's slice-of-melon smile faded. "Then you've heard about Tarleton." He sat up straight in the chair. "Listen, young Hutchinson, you know that I wish no harm to any Patriot."

Thomas sighed heavily.

"That sigh could have come from my own soul," Alexander said. "I hate what this war has done to the colony of Virginia. Why, it's ripped us apart!"

Thomas was startled. Alexander's soft, mischievous eyes were alive with anger. For a minute, he looked as Sam did when he was ranting about wanting to be a soldier.

"I consider myself to be a Virginian," Alexander said, "but because my father is a Loyalist, others here consider me an enemy." He shook his head until the neat, sand-colored queue at his neck bounced against his waistcoat collar. "I am not the enemy. I don't want to see England's mistakes repeated here! I have come to believe that government should be run for the people, not their rulers!"

Thomas stared. It was as if he were listening to a stranger.

Alexander quickly began to dig through his satchel.

"Fetch your quill pen and inkpot," he said to Thomas. "If we're going to get you admitted to the grammar school this winter, we had best get to work on your penmanship, eh?"

Thomas set about copying the day's sentence in his copybook, trying not to soak ink blobs into the paper.

But his mind was mulling over something completely different.

Has everyone traded heads when I wasn't looking? he thought. *Suddenly, Sam is content to stay here in Williamsburg just when the war is heating up. And Alexander, who always thought that after the war things would go back to the way they were before, is talking like a Patriot hothead! And there's Robert Taylor, who has suddenly become a mean father.*

"You won't win any prizes for that," Alexander said, leaning over his shoulder to look at the swoops and swirls

Thomas was making on the paper. "But at least I can read it now. Ten more times, eh?"

"I hate this," Thomas said.

"So do I." Alexander slouched down in the chair again. "I don't think there is much call for perfect handwriting in these troubled times. I would much rather be teaching you things a man is going to need to know, no matter how this war turns out."

Suddenly, he jolted up like an excited boy and grabbed Thomas's shoulder. "Does your father have a *Virginia Gazette* about?"

"You mean, the newspaper?" Thomas said.

"Yes. Does he?"

"I suppose, but—"

"Good. Before Monday I want you to read it, front to back."

"But why?" Thomas said.

"Because I want you to have every fact possible concerning what is happening today, young Hutchinson. You're going to need it."

Papa left for Yorktown again that afternoon right after dinner. He had Clayton to check on at the plantation and the warships to supervise at the docks. Thomas felt an ache in the center of his chest, and Mama smiled bravely as John Hutchinson galloped off down the dusty street that ran alongside the Palace Green. Then Mama started up the stairs in a rustle of skirts with a blur of tears in her eyes.

Thomas turned to go out the front door and off to work

at the apothecary shop when she stopped on the landing.

"Thomas?"

"Yes, ma'am?" he said from the bottom of the steps.

Virginia Hutchinson was blinking her gray eyes madly. "Don't forget that you're the man of the house again, with Papa gone."

Thomas nodded, even after she gave a wobbly smile and went on up the stairs.

At least someone thinks I'm important, he thought. *I'll show Papa—and Sam—I can be the man of the house. I can handle that.*

"*Psst!* Thomas the Tireless!"

Thomas peered into the dark hallway to see Malcolm emerging from under the stairway.

"I thought you'd never finish sayin' good-bye. I have to talk to you, lad."

Thomas felt his chest puff out. "What is it? I have things to do."

"Not before you hear this."

"If it's about a place for the Fearsome Trio to meet, I don't have time for that. I'm the man of the house now."

Even in the dim hall, he could see Malcolm's eyes snap. "This is more important than you playin' papa—"

"I'm not playing! I'm in charge now!" Thomas felt the anger sparking up his backbone. It set fire to his tongue, and he blurted out, "So why don't you go about your business? You have work to do."

Malcolm's black eyes stopped snapping. It was as if a cloud passed over them. He gave a stiff, square smile and backed toward the door. "Yes, sir," he said crisply. And he walked away.

Now Malcolm is mad at me, Thomas thought as he scuffed through the leaves to Francis's shop. *But that's what happens when you're in charge. It's what Papa would have done.*

He set his jaw squarely. But it turned to jelly when he walked into the shop. Old Francis's face was scarlet all the way up to the thin, gray hairline at the top of his head. Across the counter from him, Xavier Wormeley was flapping his jowls. Thomas nervously picked up his broom and tried to sweep without being seen.

"What makes you think you can come in here and tell me what I must do?" Francis shrieked at Xavier in his wheezy voice.

"I am an official of the court!" Xavier shouted back in his screechy one.

"You're not an official of the army! You have no right to demand that I give supplies to the hospital!"

Thomas had always thought Xavier's eyes looked like holes that had been poked into the fat of his face. They squeezed even tighter now as he nudged his tremendous belly over the countertop.

"You profess to be a Patriot," the magistrate said. "But ever since you allowed those Tory Taylors to take you in last spring, I've suspected that your loyalties have been somewhat swayed. Now I see the evidence right before me."

Francis's spectacles wobbled dangerously on the end of his nose. "What evidence?"

"Why, the fact that you will not provide the necessary medications and supplies to keep American soldiers alive!" Xavier said, straightening smugly. He swept his long, black cape out behind him with an air of importance. "I am asking you as one Patriot to another. When wounded soldiers begin to arrive, you can be sure the colonels and generals will not ask, they will demand . . . and they will take!"

And you look as if you can't wait for that to happen, Thomas thought.

"Then I shall do what I must do if and when that time comes," Francis said. He gasped for air. "But until then, I see no need to send valuable medicines to the Governor's Palace to sit on shelves gathering dust."

Xavier stuck a finger—about the size and shape of a sausage, Thomas thought—close to Francis's face. "Don't think that I am finished with you, Mr. Pickering," he said. "You haven't heard the last of this!"

With another swirl of his cape, Xavier waddled out like a duck being chased from the hen yard and slammed the door so hard behind him that the blue-and-white jars and the black bottles with their gilt-edged labels all bounced on the shelves and knocked together with a nervous clatter.

Francis took out a yellowed handkerchief and wiped his forehead and lips. "Fool," he muttered.

"Yes, sir," Thomas said automatically.

For the first time, Francis's black, bead-like eyes lit on him. "You heard all of that, I suppose."

"Yes, sir. It was hard not to."

"The man has a voice like a tin horn." Francis shook his

head, and Thomas watched the scarlet fade from his wrinkled face. Then the old man stopped and crooked his finger at Thomas.

Thomas dropped the broom and hurried over to him behind the counter. Francis hunched in close.

"Not a word of this to anyone," he said. "The towns-people will panic if they think I'll soon have no medicines for them. You're especially not to tell your father! John Hutchinson has enough to worry about."

Not tell Papa? Papa would know exactly what to do. The thought tied a knot in Thomas's stomach—until Francis poked his finger into Thomas's chest and said, "You and I can handle this alone, do you hear?"

That made Thomas feel a little better. *Maybe what I prayed to God last night, maybe that's working already. Maybe this is my chance to show Papa that I'm important, too.*

"Yes, *sir,*" Thomas said.

"It's no game, now, mind you."

"No, sir. I know."

Francis scowled into his face for a moment and then rested his clawlike hand on his shoulder.

"You're a good boy," he said. His scowl deepened. "But don't stand there gawking! Wrap up some troches for Mistress Wetherburn's heartburn and deliver them before she bothers Dr. Quincy with her tale of woe. I never saw such a woman for imaginary illnesses!"

"Where *is* Dr. Quincy this morning?" Thomas asked happily as he reached into the jar where Francis kept his ready-made drops.

"Tending to that child that got herself shot yesterday."

Thomas felt a little guilty. There had been so much going on at his house that he'd forgotten all about Patsy.

"Why do you stand there lookin' like you've had your hand in the till?" Francis said. "Get busy with those troches!"

His scalp was going crimson again, and there would have been more scolding spewing from his mouth if the front door hadn't jangled open and Caroline hadn't skipped in, cheeks flushed from the autumn air, a basket with a blue cloth over it swinging from her arm, and a pie in her hand. Francis's wizened face broke into a smile.

"Good morning, Mr. Pickering!" she said gaily. "Mama asked me to bring you this!"

She pushed the pie forward—mince—still steaming from the oven. Thomas took a sniff, and drool formed at the corners of his mouth.

"You can put your nostrils to rest, Hutchinson," Francis said, peering at him over his spectacles. "You won't be getting any of this, at least not until your work's done."

Thomas dove under the counter for a ball of string, knocking over a mortar and pestle and a jar of Epsom salts in the process. Caroline giggled.

"That's one of the reasons I'm here," she said. "Tom's work, I mean."

"Oh?" the old apothecary said.

"Mama wants to know if I could go along on Tom's deliveries today, and we could perhaps ask in some of the shops along the way if anyone knows anything about Patsy, our little lost girl."

Thomas ventured a peek over the counter. Francis was beaming down at Caroline and shaking his head.

"How can I ever refuse you anything, Mistress Caroline?" he said. "Of course you can." He darted a fierce glance in Thomas's direction. "Just see that you make those deliveries, boy, and remember what I said."

Thomas nodded and followed Caroline out the door. Her eyes danced with excitement.

"What was he talking about?" she asked. "What did he say to you?"

Out of habit, Thomas started to answer. He always told Caroline, and now Malcolm, everything. They were part of the Fearsome Trio.

But he set his jaw and chewed his lip.

"Well?" Caroline said.

"It's business," he said. "Nothing you would be interested in."

He glanced at her sideways, ready for her next question. Caroline never gave up easily. But her eyes clouded a bit as she stared at him. Thomas's stomach knotted up, and he said quickly, "Did you get into bad trouble with your father last night?"

Now it was Caroline's turn to chew her lip. "No," she said.

"He seemed awfully angry. I've never seen him like that before."

For a moment, it looked as if she were going to tell him. But as soon as she opened her mouth, she closed it and rearranged the basket on her arm. "It's nothing you would be interested in," she said and walked on.

Thomas felt that sting again. One minute he'd been talking

to his best friend, and the next he was trailing a stranger down the street. *I can't tell you my secret,* he wanted to shout to her. *But that doesn't mean you can't tell me yours.*

Instead, he ran to catch up with her and nudged the arm where she held the basket. "What's in there?" he asked.

She swallowed hard and said, "Just Martha."

Everything else flipped out of Thomas's mind. "Why did you bring her?"

"Shhh!" Caroline said. "You'll hurt her feelings!"

"That cat doesn't have any feelings," Thomas said, whispering just in case.

"You just never know when you might need Martha." Caroline peeked under the blue cloth and poked a finger in. "Isn't that right, kitty?"

Thomas winced at the thought of putting *his* finger into that basket. Martha had never sunk her teeth or claws into his flesh, but he'd seen some of her victims. Even Malcolm had a healthy respect for her.

"Come on," Caroline said. "Let's find Patsy's parents."

But it wasn't a successful afternoon. Everyone was curious about a stranger coming to town, but no one knew anything about her. Not the blacksmith or the printer or Elizabeth Tarpley in the general store. The same with the milliner, the cabinetmaker, and the weaver.

As Caroline and Thomas worked their way from one end of the Duke of Gloucester Street to the other, their spirits began to dive.

"It's as if Patsy was dropped into Peggy Cheswell's stable

from the sky," Thomas growled when they left the leather-smith's. Red-whiskered Guy Howard had been as smiling and friendly as usual, but neither that, nor the cinnamon candies Mistress Tarpley had tucked into their hands at the general store, nor the free *Virginia Gazette* the printer had given Thomas, could chase away the shadows that had fallen across their minds.

"Why did you ask for that newspaper, Tom?" Caroline asked as they headed down Nassau Street.

"Alexander told me to read it from front to back for lessons on Monday."

Caroline gave him a sideways look. "That sounds like fun."

"I guess so," Thomas said.

"You don't know what it's like being left out of school, Tom. You're so lucky to be a boy!"

"You know how to read. Why don't you just read the newspaper if you want to?"

Caroline considered that as they turned the corner at Nassau and headed up Francis Street. They both peered up at the Public Hospital, looked at each other, and quickened their steps. Surely there was no need to ask there.

Patsy didn't look insane to me, Thomas assured himself. He tried not to consider that he had never seen an insane person, so he wouldn't know what one looked like anyway.

"Let's try the gunsmith's shop," he said. "It's closer to the edge of town, and it's near Peggy Cheswell's."

Caroline's face brightened, and they hurried under the canopy of fire-colored trees to the corner of Blair and Francis Streets.

Caroline started to skip, still swinging the basket full of Martha beside her.

She's forgotten that I shut her out of my secret with Francis, Thomas thought. His heart felt lighter, until they reached the steps of the gunsmith's yellow shop and heard voices cracking like shots from inside.

"You're a thief!" shot one angry voice.

"Put down that weapon!" another fired back. "Put it down—before you shoot someone!"

✝ ✤ ✝

Chapter Five

Thomas stared at Caroline. In her eyes he could see the same terror he could feel in his own. Her wind-flushed cheeks went porridge-white.

"Put it down, Walter," said one of the voices inside the shop. The voice was calm in a stiff way, as if the man were talking to a child.

"You're a thief, George Fenton!" the other voice said. *"You're* trying to steal from *me.* Why shouldn't *I* steal from *you?"*

"Drop it, Walter!"

Before Thomas and Caroline could move, the green door was flung open. A young man of about 20 hurled himself down the steps. The long gun he was carrying stuck out away from his body, and its barrel grazed Caroline's back and knocked her against the porch railing. The basket slid off her arm and bounced down the steps, spilling out a surprised and disgruntled mass of hissing orange fur.

"Get him, Martha!" Caroline screamed.

The cat bared two rows of needle-sharp teeth in a snarl and then threw herself, claws poised, at the young man's elbow. He let out a howl Thomas was sure could be heard at Wetherburn's Tavern. His hands flew up, the gun hit the ground, and he took off toward Francis Street with Martha wrapped around his arm. It took him two blocks to shake her off.

As he disappeared around the corner, the shop door opened again. This time it was George Fenton who stepped warily out onto the porch.

From the first time Thomas had seen him, the gunsmith had reminded him of a beaver. He was a slightly round person with rich brown hair that lay close to his head and a pair of lively eyes that lay close to each other. The feature that stood out the most was his teeth, which extended over his lower lip and forced it to sink into his chin. He wasn't funny-looking to Thomas, though, maybe because he was always so serious and busy.

But right now he looked angry as he retrieved the gun from the ground and inspected it like a mother picking up a hurt child.

"Did he hurt it?" Caroline said. She scooped up Martha, who had returned triumphantly, and dropped her back into the basket.

"No, lucky for him," George Fenton said. "Took it right off the wall pegs, he did, and was going to run off with it! Simple fool, that one. I'd hate to see him with a gun even if he could afford one. All of Williamsburg would have to go into hiding."

Thomas and Caroline exchanged glances. He could tell from the gleam in her eyes that she was going to ask a thousand questions. If George Fenton were like everyone else in town, he'd answer every one.

"Who was that man?" she said as they followed George into the shop.

He went straight to his worktable, but he answered as he carved away at the beginnings of a gun stock. "Walter Clark," he said. "He just married Lydia Rowley. They've moved in down the street."

"Why did he call you a thief?" Caroline said, settling herself on a stool at the end of the worktable and smoothing her petticoat over her knees.

Thomas leaned awkwardly against the wall and crossed his arms.

"He claims I'm charging too much for my guns," George said. He picked up the maple stock and blew some shavings off it before he went on. "He said he was going off to war and wanted a gun to leave with his new bride to protect her while she was home alone. When I told him how much it would cost, he exploded like a musket ball and told me I was stealing the citizens of Williamsburg blind." George rested his buck teeth on his lower lip for a moment. "I tried to explain to him that it takes 400 hours to make a weapon, but he just ranted that I was trying to rob him. I don't understand it. Lydia Rowley's family is wealthy. There should be no shortage of money in that house."

Thomas had caught only a glimpse of Walter Clark as he'd lurched down the steps. He could remember his red, almost raw-looking skin, especially on the hands that had clutched the gun. His reddish-brown hair had stuck out in all directions as if it had never seen a brush or comb.

But it was his eyes Thomas remembered best. They'd looked painfully blue against their bloodshot background, and they hadn't been still for even a second.

"We have a question for you, Mr. Fenton—Tom and I," Caroline was saying. "Have you seen or heard anything about a lost girl, about eight years old?"

George didn't say anything, and Thomas began looking around the shop. The walls were lined with peg strips hung with polished shotguns, pistols, muskets, and rifles. Thomas didn't know much about guns. There had never been any reason to. But in the last two days, he'd seen two different weapons being waved about by people who probably didn't know any more than he did about them. And he'd had a conversation with Alexander about dragoons, the horseback pistol shooters. The sight of all these guns waiting to fire their bullets—by citizens or soldiers—made him chew his thumbnail.

"No, I've heard nothing about a lost young one," George Fenton said finally. "Is this girl a friend of yours?"

"Not exactly. We're just trying to help her—Tom and I. She was accidentally shot in the foot by Peggy Cheswell yesterday, and no one knows who she is. She won't talk."

"Probably had the voice scared right out of her," George said dryly. "I'd be frightened, too, if that old woman came after me with a gun. I should have known better than to sell it to her, but she said she needed it for protection, what with the Tarleton raids coming closer." He sucked on his lower lip until Thomas thought he would swallow it. "I always thought I was doing a good thing by providing well-made weapons for hunting and soldiering, but now I'm not so sure. It seems the whole colony's gone mad."

He continued to mutter to himself as Caroline and Thomas slipped out of the shop. The day was graying into evening.

"I think we've run out of places to ask," Thomas said.

Caroline gnawed thoughtfully at a fingernail. "Maybe Mr. Fenton is right about one thing," she said.

"What's that?"

"Patsy might have just been too frightened to speak yesterday, but perhaps she'll talk today. Mistress Cheswell's is just up the street."

Dr. Quincy was packing his things back into his bag when Peggy Cheswell ushered them into her spare bed-room—all the while mumbling, "I didn't mean to. You know I didn't mean to!"

Nicholas presented Patsy to Caroline and Thomas with a flourish of his arm.

"You look so well!" Caroline said to her. She crossed the room to the four-poster cherrywood bed with its red-and-white flowered canopy and curtain. Patsy was propped up against a mountain of cushions that matched the one that supported her bandaged foot.

She looks much different than she did yesterday, Thomas thought. Her thick, dark hair had been neatly rebraided and tied with ribbons the same cobalt blue as the nightgown that swallowed her. Although she didn't smile, her face looked rested and calm, but her green eyes were still sad.

"Is she all better?" Caroline said to Nicholas.

"She will be," the doctor said. "She's strong for being so tiny. A fighter."

Caroline made herself at home on the side of the bed. "Does it hurt much?"

Patsy didn't answer.

"I'm sure it does, though she doesn't say," Dr. Quincy said. "They tell me that when you're shot, it feels like you've been clubbed with a tree branch. Musket balls are soft, and they mushroom out when they hit things."

Caroline put her hand up to her mouth.

"God was with Mistress Patsy, though," Nicholas said calmly. "It didn't hit the bone and shatter it. She'll be walking again in no time at the rate she's going."

"I'm really glad," Caroline said, nodding for all she was worth. "We all are." She shot a look at Thomas, who nodded, too. To Patsy, she added, "Will you tell us your name? And where you come from?"

But instead of answering, Patsy craned her neck to look beyond Caroline, beyond Thomas, and beyond the doorway.

"What's she looking for?" Thomas whispered to Dr. Quincy.

"I have no idea."

"I think I know," Caroline said. "She's probably looking for Malcolm."

Patsy's face lit up like the candle on the windowsill, and for a moment, Thomas thought she was going to scramble out of bed and dash for the door.

"Whoa there," Nicholas said gently. "You're not quite ready for that yet!"

Caroline set about plumping up Patsy's pillows and smoothing out her quilt. Nicholas turned to Thomas and whispered, "See if you can't get young Malcolm here, eh? I think he'd be good medicine for her."

Thomas squared his shoulders. "He has free time after supper. I'll send him then."

Malcolm will do it, of course, he added in his mind. *He knows I'm not fooling about things, now that I'm in charge.*

"Interesting, eh, how she took to him?" Nicholas said.

"I suppose, sir," Thomas said. He caught Caroline's eye and motioned for her to hurry. He knew he had better get back to the apothecary shop before old Francis got himself wound up like a spring.

"I have to go now, Patsy," Caroline said. "But I'll be back, don't you worry."

Something shimmered through Patsy's big eyes, but she didn't smile, and of course she didn't answer. Caroline leaned over and kissed her softly on the cheek. Thomas turned and bolted from the room before Caroline could suggest that he do the same.

He found Malcolm in the kitchen building that evening just before supper. He was setting Esther's iron pots on the coals of the fire so she could heap more embers on the lids to make meat pies. Esther looked at Thomas with frosty eyes. Malcolm didn't look up at all.

Thomas marched over to the fire. "Malcolm," he said, "Patsy wants to see you."

Malcolm jolted up from the hearth. "Did she talk?"

"No, but we could all tell it's you she wants. You're to go right after supper."

"Well, well!" Esther said. She stood up straight from her pot and put her hands on her vast hips. The old eyes glittered at Thomas. "Look who's givin' orders now!"

It was hard not to wither under her gaze, but Thomas tried to stand taller. "I am," he said. "I'm in charge with Papa gone."

Esther's eyes bulged as she drew her mouth into an O.

"It's true!" he said. "Mama said so."

"No one told me!" she said. "And until they do—"

"Esther," said a voice from the corner by the window.

For the first time, Thomas saw that Esther's husband, old Otis, was sitting in a chair, whittling a piece of wood. They all stared at him. Otis rarely spoke, but when he did he was worth listening to.

"What?" Esther snapped at him.

But that was apparently all Otis intended to say, because he bent his head of thinning hair over his wood piece and remained silent. Esther, however, had gotten some message, because she tossed her cap-covered head at Thomas and maneuvered herself over to her husband. She picked up a bowl of apples, said "humph," and set to peeling with a vengeance.

Those apples will be rotten before they get to the table, Thomas thought.

He turned to share a grin about that with Malcolm. But the servant boy was taking off his apron and running his hand through his hair as if he were off to a fire.

"I'll go now," he said, and then looked sharply at Thomas. "If that be meetin' your approval, sir."

Thomas felt a pang of hurt. There was an edge in Malcolm's voice Thomas hadn't heard there in a long time. *But I can't let that bother me,* he told himself. *I have things to prove now.*

"Yes, go," he said.

Malcolm took off out the door and vanished into the gray evening. Thomas followed at a more dignified pace, worthy of the man of the house.

"He's gettin' pretty big for his breeches, don't you think?" he heard Esther say from behind the door.

Thomas didn't hear an answer from Otis, but he asked himself the same question. *Am I acting too big for my breeches? Would Papa think so?*

He walked to the house, a little less dignified, wishing that Papa were there.

But no, he told himself. *I can do this by myself. I can.*

✝ ✦ ✝

Chapter Six

Thomas woke up the next morning, Saturday, to a fresh-apple-tart smell wafting up from below. He lay in the early-morning chill for a few minutes, snuggled under his quilt, before the sleep cleared out of his head. Then he realized that it could not be Esther's cooking he was smelling. This might be worth getting out of bed for.

There were no lessons on Saturdays, and Malcolm had long since taken over most of the morning chores, so Thomas went straight to the dining room. But there were no porringers and spoons set for breakfast. There was only Mama putting tiny golden-brown pies and ginger cakes sparkling with sugar into a basket. Thomas's mouth watered immediately.

"Where did these come from?" he said, hungrily eyeing two round-topped cakes as she placed them inside.

Mama looked at him innocently. "Why, from Esther. Who else?"

Thomas leaned over to inspect a tart, and his mother laughed like a tinkling bell. "I'm teasing you, Thomas. God bless dear Esther, she's been a joy to this family for generations. But the woman could burn water."

Thomas nodded, although he wasn't sure he could agree to Esther's being a "joy."

"Betsy Taylor has been generous again," Mama went on. "She says their cook bakes far too much for them to eat before the mice get to it."

By now Thomas's stomach was growling the way Martha did before she erupted from Caroline's basket. He watched enviously as Mama tucked the last baked goody away and covered the whole lot with a snowy white napkin.

"Where are these going?" he asked.

"I was hoping you would take them to Sam for me. He is forever complaining about the food at the college, and he's studying so hard this term—metaphysics and moral philosophy and such things." She gave a little shiver and then laughed at herself. "I *am* going on, aren't I? I'm proud of Samuel. He's smart and handsome and a fine gentleman. Let's see that he gets a treat, shall we?"

Samuel is working so hard, Thomas thought a little bitterly as he took the basket and headed across the Palace Green. *Samuel is smart and handsome and a fine gentleman. Let's see that Samuel gets a treat.*

He had to shake his head as he hurried on toward the College of William and Mary, which watched over Williamsburg from the end of the Duke of Gloucester Street.

It's all right, he told himself. *She'll know soon. They'll all know soon that I'm up there with Sam and Clayton.*

Then he reached into the basket and pulled out the plumpest apple tart he'd ever seen. It went into his mouth immediately.

The college was made up of three large buildings, all built of pinkish-colored bricks with black specks that made them look to Thomas like rice pudding. There were Brafferton Hall, the Main Building, and the President's House, and they looked down at him in a superior way out of their many-windowed eyes. The lawn was dotted with young men in the required long black robes and black cocked hats, rushing about with books tucked under their flowing sleeves. Thomas headed for Sam's room in the Main Building.

It was quiet in the dark, chilly hall. The boys were required to study on Saturdays, and Thomas wondered if Sam were reading moral philosophy, whatever that was.

When he got to the big wooden door of Sam's room, he was surprised to hear Sam talking to someone. He was even more surprised when he recognized the other voice. Thomas slipped over to the doorway next door and flattened himself in the darkness.

"That isn't important," the other voice said. "Most soldiers now wear anything they can get their hands on. Providing a gun is the problem. Most have to trade a horse for a musket when they get there."

Thomas heard Sam laugh quietly. "After last summer, I'm through with horses, I can tell you that."

Their voices grew lower, and Thomas inched closer to hear. The basket scraped against the wall.

"Shhh!" Sam whispered from inside the room. "Did you hear that?"

"I did."

"You'd better leave. Wear my robe so you won't be noticed. Leave it in the bushes, and I'll get it later."

Thomas plastered himself inside the next doorway again and held his breath. Almost as soon as he did, Sam's door opened and a slim figure slid out and disappeared down the hall the other way, with Sam's black robe trailing out behind him. It was Alexander Taylor.

Thomas nearly let the basket fall from his hand. His head was spinning. *What was Alexander doing here? Sam can barely stand the sight of Alexander. That's why he tried to get him run out of town last summer. And Alexander hates him for doing it!*

To Thomas, the silent but furious feud between Sam and Alexander was the worst part of the Patriot-Loyalist battle. And now here was Alexander, sneaking out of Sam's room.

Just then Sam's door opened again, and Sam poked his head out and scanned the hall. When his eyes found Thomas, he gave a snort, and his face broke into a handsome smile.

"Playing spy, little brother?"

"No . . . I . . . I brought you some cakes and tarts!" Thomas said, thrusting the basket out in front of him.

Sam peered up and down the hall, eyes bulging. "Oh!" he whispered. "I see! I understand the British have been lurking about for days, ready to steal baked goods from unsuspecting Patriots!"

Thomas felt the angry prickles on the back of his neck again.

"Here!" he said, dropping the basket with a thud. "Mama says to send the basket home when you're finished."

He started to stomp by, but Sam grabbed him by the front of his brown holland vest and chuckled. "I'm sorry, little brother. I didn't mean to offend you. You just looked for all the world as if you had something to hide."

"I'm not the one with something to hide!" Thomas blurted out.

Sam stared at him for a moment, then glanced toward the staircase where Alexander had disappeared.

"Oh," he said. "Perhaps you ought to come inside." He nodded toward the basket with his blue eyes twinkling. "Why don't you bring that with you?"

Thomas was still scowling as he followed Sam into his spare, white cubicle of a room and once again dropped the basket, this time on Sam's lumpy bed.

"So you saw Alexander leaving," Sam said.

"Of course I saw him! I may be but 11 years old, but I'm not blind!"

Sam raised a honey-colored eyebrow. "My, but you've turned hostile, Thomas!"

Thomas glowered at him.

"All right," Sam said. "I should have known you would spot him, smart as you're getting." He ran his hand through his curly blond hair and looked at Thomas with a lopsided smile. "Can we sit down and talk? I'll share some of these treats with you—provided Esther didn't make them. If she did, we'll have a game of shuffleboard with them, eh?"

Thomas shrugged and sank down into Sam's straight-backed desk chair. Sam selected an apple tart and stretched out on his bed. He chewed thoughtfully for a minute before he started in.

"I hoped no one would see Alexander here. In fact, I told him we should meet elsewhere from now on, and it seems I was right."

Thomas felt an uneasy stirring in his stomach. "Why *was* he here? I thought you . . . I thought you hated him."

Sam put up his hand. "I never said I hated *him*. He's a fine fellow, actually. Nearly as smart as I am!" He gave a wink to let Thomas know he was teasing, but Thomas still frowned. He wasn't going to be thrown off the track by Sam's charm this time. Sam cleared his throat. "No, I just hated what he stood for. Loyalism and all that."

"*Stood* for?" Thomas said. "He still does, doesn't he?"

Sam sat up and put down the tart. His teasing face grew serious. "Last summer, I thought you would keep any secret I told you, but I was wrong."

"That's not fair!" Thomas cried.

"Now hear me out. You were right not to keep it to yourself then. But this is different. No one can know about this. No one."

Thomas squirmed impatiently in the chair. "If you're going to tell me, then tell me."

Sam considered it for a moment longer before he scooted

to the edge of the bed and leaned close to Thomas. "Alexander has become a Patriot," he said.

"What?" Thomas said. He searched Sam's eyes for traces of teasing, but there were none. "That can't be true. Caroline would have told me!"

"She doesn't know. None of the Taylors know."

"Why?"

Sam gave a hard laugh. "Isn't that obvious, little brother? Robert Taylor is still as much a Loyalist as he ever was, but Alexander has seen the light. He can see a new and better world emerging through freedom, just like the rest of us. He wants to be a citizen of the great republic of humanity we're building here in America."

Sam's eyes shone. Thomas remembered the same light shining in his teacher's face just yesterday.

"Alexander wants to help the Patriot cause," Sam said, "and he can probably do that best by pretending to remain on the side of the British."

Thomas felt his mouth drop open. "You mean . . . he's a spy?"

"He could become one. That's all I really know right now."

Thomas was confused. "But that still doesn't tell me why he came here," he said.

Sam smiled. "Haven't you ever had a secret? Only it wasn't any fun just having it yourself? You wanted to share it with someone—someone who would be bowled over like a milk jug by it?"

"Yes," Thomas said slowly. He'd wanted to tell his family about Patsy. And he'd almost told Caroline about Francis's fight with Xavier Wormeley. He supposed that was a good enough answer, yet it sounded like a story in which something important had been left out.

"There you have it." Sam slapped his knee and reached for his tart again. "But you have to promise not to tell anyone—especially Caroline."

Thomas went to work on his fingernails. Sam was watching him carefully.

"You can't keep secrets from your little Loyalist friend, can you?"

"I can if I have to!" Thomas said.

Sam looked him full in the eyes. "You have to this time. It's for the Patriots. What's more important than that?"

"Well, nothing," Thomas said uneasily.

"Good." Sam stood up. "We're in this together then."

Thomas stood up, too. His eyes were almost level with Sam's.

"Look there," Sam said, flashing a smile, "you're nearly as tall as I am. I know I can trust you."

Thomas nodded and puffed out his chest.

✢ ⬦ ✢

Chapter Seven

As Thomas trudged back down the Duke of Gloucester Street toward the Palace Green, he didn't feel quite so sure of himself. Thoughts were passing through his mind like the clouds that scudded overhead. He couldn't really catch hold of any of them.

Alexander, a Patriot?

Alexander risking visiting Sam in his room at the college, just to share a secret?

And me not being able to tell Caroline? How can I look at her without her knowing I'm hiding something? I can't even keep her from knowing I have cinnamon candy in my pouch!

He wished he could ask the people he looked up to most — Papa, Sam, even Alexander himself.

The bells of Bruton Parish Church pealed out noontide, and Thomas looked up at the steeple that pointed to the sky as if it were showing the way to God. There was God to go to, of course.

But I can't run to God like a whining ninny every time things get hard, he thought. *I told God I would do whatever it takes, and I'm doing it.*

"Tom!" a voice chirped. "There you are!"

Thomas lurched to a stop as if he'd been shot. Caroline skipped toward him from the direction of the printer's shop. She was carrying a newspaper.

"I've been looking all over for you!"

"Oh," he said. He tried not to look into her brown eyes— which, of course, she noticed right away.

"What are you up to, Tom?" she demanded. And then a gleam came into her eyes. "Don't tell me. I already know. You have gone and found out who Patsy's family is without even taking me along."

Thomas tried not to tremble too hard with relief as he shook his head. "No!" he said. "I wasn't even . . . well, no, I didn't find them."

"Why did you go looking without me? I thought we were partners."

"We are!" Thomas said quickly. "And I wasn't . . ."

She waited, sandy eyebrows arched.

Thomas groped for something to say and finally pointed to the newspaper. "What's that for?" he said.

Caroline tossed her hair back over the shoulders of her red cape. "I'm going to read it."

"Oh," Thomas said.

He realized with a pang that he hadn't done his assignment

for Alexander yet. There was so much to think about these days, not the least of which was Alexander himself becoming a Patriot. Thomas started to walk to keep Caroline from pulling that thought right off his face.

"Where shall we ask about Patsy today?" he said.

That seemed to chase all other ideas from Caroline's head. "I think we should start with Peggy Cheswell's neighbors," she said, leading him down Duke of Gloucester toward Queen Street. "Patsy couldn't have traveled very far on foot before Mistress Cheswell shot her. She's too little."

Thomas agreed. He would have agreed to anything to get Caroline's mind off where he'd been and what he'd been doing—and what he'd just heard in Sam's room. But as they went from clapboard house to clapboard house, the questions wouldn't leave him alone: *What had Sam and Alexander really been up to? Those things I heard them say to each other, what did they mean?*

"Tom, you haven't heard a thing I've said," Caroline said, interrupting his thoughts.

"Yes, I have," Thomas said.

"Then what's your answer?"

"My answer? My answer is . . . yes."

That was usually a safe answer with Caroline. And it appeared to be the right one this time, because she grabbed his hand and practically dragged him up Francis Street. She led him up the front walk of a gray house with a shutter that hung like a broken arm from its hinges.

"Caroline!" Thomas whispered hoarsely. He dug his heels into the stones. "I think this is Walter Clark's house!"

Caroline stared at it for a moment. "Oh," she said. "We can't knock on his door! He might point a gun at us!"

"He doesn't have a gun, remember?"

"He's probably stolen one by now!" Thomas started backing down the walkway.

"Come on, Tom! No one we've talked to today knows anything about Patsy. We have to find out something, and we can't skip anyone."

"What makes you think these people are going to know anything?"

"What makes you think they're not?"

Thomas set his square jaw stubbornly. "I'm not going up to that door."

"Good, then," Caroline said. "I'll go by myself."

She turned on her heel and marched up the narrow brick steps to the door. A picture flashed across Thomas's mind—of Walter Clark hurling himself from the gunsmith's shop, hair on end, mouth twitching, eyes like a wild animal's.

"All right, I'll come with you," he said. "But at the first sign of trouble, run!"

"Of course," she said.

As she knocked on the door, Thomas wiggled inside his shirt. Caroline was always ready for adventure. She never seemed to have a thousand doubts as he did. Thomas looked around to be sure there was a good place to hide when they had to make a run for it.

Caroline knocked, but no one came to the door.

"Let's go," Thomas said from the bottom of the steps.

"There's no one home."

"Yes, there is! I heard someone playing the harpsichord. Shhh!"

Caroline pressed her ear against the door, and Thomas glanced nervously over his shoulder.

"Someone's coming!" she hissed.

The front door began to open and stopped at only a crack. *A crack big enough for a gun barrel!* Thomas thought.

But Caroline stuck her nose right into the opening and said, "Hello, there. Are you Lydia?"

In spite of himself, Thomas edged a little closer. He had never seen Lydia Rowley Clark. He wondered what a woman who married someone as strange as Walter would look like.

The face that was squeezed between the door and its frame made him think at once of a mouse he might find in the stable. Her hair was thin and brown, and her frightened eyes quivered when she said, "Yes."

Caroline put out her hand. Lydia pulled hers back from the door and started to close it.

"Oh, no, please!" Caroline said. "We just want to ask you a question."

But the door clicked shut, and Thomas heard a bolt come down from the inside.

"She's hiding something," Caroline said. She crossed her arms over her chest as if it were all decided.

"She looked afraid to me," Thomas said.

Caroline sighed. "If she knows anything, we'll never find out."

They trailed off down the street without talking. As Caroline walked, she looked straight ahead, and Thomas sneaked a glance at her. Her face made him kick miserably at a stone. Her eyes were swimming.

"You aren't going to cry, are you?" he said.

"No!" she said. But she smeared off the tears that trickled down her cheeks.

"Yes, you are."

"Well, why shouldn't I? Wouldn't you hate it if you were lost and couldn't find your family and couldn't tell anyone who they were?"

Thomas looked down at his shoe buckles. "I suppose."

"We have to find them, Tom!" Caroline's lower lip quivered, and she bit hard at it. But she couldn't keep her eyes from spilling over or her face from twisting as if it hurt.

Thomas wanted to punch something. He hated to see her cry.

"All right," he said. "We'll find them. I promise you, we will."

Caroline gazed into his eyes for so long that Thomas had to look at his toes again.

"If you say so, Tom, then I know it's going to happen," she said. "Because you would never lie to me."

Thomas felt his face going as red as one of the maple leaves that floated down around them.

"Let's go see Patsy," he said in a hurry. "That will cheer you up."

Caroline nodded happily and swiped at her tears. Thomas felt as if he were suddenly carrying all of Williamsburg on his back.

When they arrived at Peggy Cheswell's, the shriveled old lady was lighting the candles in the windows.

"Someone else has beaten you here," she said, nodding up toward Patsy's room. "And I'm glad of it," she added with a whine. "She was getting mighty restless."

Out of breath and windblown, they climbed the stairs and poked their heads in the door. There by Patsy's bed, looking oddly out of place amid the flowered curtains and Patsy's lacy cap, stood Malcolm. Patsy was smiling her crooked-toothed smile up at him as if he were the only person in the room. *Maybe even the world,* Thomas thought.

"Malcolm!" Caroline said as she skipped over to Patsy's bed. "Guess what?"

"What, lassie?" Malcolm looked down at her with a square smile.

"Tom has promised that we'll find Patsy's family. We are going to try everything."

Malcolm's smile faded, and his gaze bored into Thomas. His eyes were so cold that Thomas felt a shiver go up his spine.

"There's no need for that," Malcolm said. "I'll be findin' them myself."

Caroline's eyebrows puckered. "But Malcolm, Tom said—"

"Thank you," Malcolm said stiffly, "but I'll be fine."

Caroline blinked from one of them to the other.

No, you won't, Thomas thought angrily. *I'll find them.*

On Monday, when Thomas asked if there were any deliveries to make, Francis glared at him over the top of his teetering spectacles.

"No!" he barked in his high-pitched voice. "Every time I send you out on a delivery lately, you're away long enough to have gone out into the fields, picked the herbs, and dried them!" He poked a bony finger close to Thomas's nose. "Cold weather is coming on, and this town will have every illness known to man, and then some. Mistress Wetherburn alone will have us hopping to keep in enough bugloss root for her cough."

By now his head was red halfway up his scalp, and he hunched over the columbine he was making into lotion for sore throats. "Running all over town looking for some miserable orphan's parents while I have sick people to tend to," he muttered.

Thomas chewed on the inside of his mouth and headed for the cellar for more dried herbs. He felt heavy as he reached up to yank the crinkly leaves and stems from the ceiling where Francis had hung them.

How will I get out to ask about Patsy? he thought. He sneezed as a tuft of horseheal floated past his nose. *I have to do this for Caroline, to make up for keeping all these secrets from her. And to show Malcolm, too.*

"Hutchinson!" Francis called out. "Come wrap up this woundwort tea!"

He shook off his thoughts and flew up to the shop, where he ducked under the counter for some newspaper.

"So," Francis said, "did you ever find out who that young girl belonged to? The one who was shot at Peggy Cheswell's?"

"No, sir," Thomas said, still crouched below, searching for string.

"I've asked everyone who's come in here. No one knows a thing, though they're all quick to offer their opinions. Some say she's a Loyalist separated from her parents while she was escaping from some Patriot town. Others swear she is a Patriot on the run from one of those Tarleton raids."

"Why don't you ask Alexander Taylor?" said a voice from the doorway. "He seems to know everything about *both* sides these days!"

Thomas froze under the counter. It was the unmistakable voice of Xavier Wormeley.

✛ ⋅✛⋅ ✛

Chapter Eight

"**W**hat's this now?" Thomas heard old Francis ask. "You're accusing Alexander Taylor of being a *Patriot?*"

Thomas slowly stood up from his place behind the counter and muttered, "I better get to sweeping the cellar." Anything to get out from under the stern, suspicious gaze of Mr. Wormeley. Thomas walked to the stairway that led down to the cellar. After a few steps down the stairs, he stopped so he could take in every word.

Xavier seemed hardly to notice him leave the room. Instead, he said, loudly enough for anyone in Yorktown to hear, "I don't know what to believe anymore! Young Taylor still *claims* to be a Loyalist, though why he would want to be is still beyond me."

"Especially with you lurking in his shadow all the time," Francis put in.

Thomas stifled a giggle from his place on the stairway. He could imagine Francis's head going scarlet, and Xavier's beady eyes almost squinting shut.

"You wouldn't be so quick to poke fun at me, Mr. Pickering," said the magistrate, "if you knew what I know."

We're going to know any minute now, Thomas thought to himself. *He couldn't keep a secret if the whole Patriot cause depended on it.*

"I am holding my breath," Francis said.

"I have half a mind not to tell you, beings how you're so full of yourself, Pickering." Xavier cleared his throat importantly. "But it is my duty to inform every Williamsburg citizen." Again he coughed. There was a long pause.

"For heaven's sake, Wormeley, let's have it!" Francis cried. "I have work to do here."

But Xavier wasn't going to be cheated out of his moment. There was yet another dramatic silence before he said, "It has come to my attention that Alexander Taylor has been reading certain Patriot literature. I was told this in great excitement by a certain citizen who thought I would be overjoyed by the news."

"Well, aren't you?" Francis said gruffly.

Xavier gave what Thomas always called a know-it-all laugh.

"Ah, you know so little of wartime intrigue, Mr. Pickering. Let me enlighten you."

His voice grew so low that Thomas could barely hear him. He crept quietly to the top of the stairs and peeked around the corner. Xavier was leaning over the counter, belly squashed on its top. Francis was glaring so hard through his spectacles that Thomas was sure he would bore holes through the glass.

"It is my suspicion," Xavier whispered, "that young Alexander Taylor is a spy."

Thomas had to plaster both hands over his mouth to keep from crying out. His heart began to race.

"What?" Francis spluttered. "For the British?"

"Well, who else?" Xavier said with a snort. "Surely not *our* side! Who would trust him?"

"I'd trust him with my life!" Francis cried.

"I'll not trust him with mine! Many times I have tried to drive him and his lousy Loyalist family out of this Patriot town, and John Hutchinson and his followers have stopped me." Xavier drew in a noisy sniff. "They all said the Taylors were quiet and hurt no one and should be allowed to stay. But this—they can't argue with this, Pickering! Now young Taylor is acting as secret service for the king!"

"Get out of here, Wormeley," Francis said in disgust. "And take your ridiculous ideas with you."

Xavier tried to draw himself up to a great height, but his chubby neck wouldn't let him. As a result, his eyebrows threatened to take flight from his face. "He's a traitor, as bad as that Benedict Arnold."

"You're a fool!"

"Remember that you are talking to your magistrate, Mr. Pickering!"

"And what of it?" Francis said. He picked up his mortar and pestle and went back to work.

Thomas took a few steps down the stairs and leaned against the wall with his head spinning. It couldn't be! Sam had said Alexander was a spy—but for the *Patriots*. Xavier cleared his throat again, and Thomas held his breath to listen.

"That is not the only reason I came here," the magistrate said. "I have a written order for you, Mr. Pickering."

"What's this?"

There was a crackling of paper, and then a gasp from Francis. Thomas thought surely he'd keeled over, until he began to shriek.

"What is the meaning of this, Wormeley?"

"You've just read it. You are to turn over all of your medicines for use in the military hospital in the Governor's Palace."

"I will do nothing of the sort!"

"I think you will, unless you want to be taken to the jail. You see there that it is signed by a military official of high rank."

"I see some chicken scratching here. How do I know this is a genuine signature?"

"Disobey this order and you'll find out soon enough," Xavier said. He was about to give one of his know-it-all laughs again, Thomas knew.

Thomas himself felt far from laughter. He balled both hands into fists and squeezed them.

"If you are smart, Pickering," Xavier went on, "you will pack up these items at once and have them delivered to the Governor's Palace by nightfall tomorrow."

"I can read!" Francis said. His voice had wound up to an earsplitting pitch.

"The officers have been more than generous in allowing you enough time to gather—"

"*Generous?!*" The word exploded from Francis like a cannonball. "I'll be out of business within the week if I give all of this to the hospital!"

"Then you should have doubled your supply so you'd have enough to sell to your patients," Xavier said. He sounded like Esther when she scolded Thomas. "You cannot say I didn't warn you."

Francis's reply came out low and threatening. "Get out."

"I will for now. But if I do not see medicines arriving at the Governor's Palace—"

"I said, get *out.*"

Xavier did—hurriedly. Thomas peeked around the corner in time to see his wide form steer itself out the door and waddle down the steps.

They both stared until the fat figure disappeared into Raleigh Tavern.

"He's an idiot!" Francis slapped both bony hands down on the countertop and glowered down at them. When he looked up, he saw Thomas. "Forget about that package of woundwort," he said.

"Are you going to give the medicines to the hospital?" Thomas asked.

Francis's spectacles wobbled on his nose. "What choice do I have? You begin with the cellar. . . ."

Thomas spent the rest of the afternoon downstairs, collecting black bottles of liquids, jars of troches, and pots of syrups. As the shelves gave up their cloves for curing toothaches and licorice root for coughs and rattlesnake root for fevers, Thomas tried to sort through his confusion.

The Patriot cause is good, he thought. *Papa says if we win the war, all Americans will be free and equal.*

He frowned as he dropped a jar of hartshorn into the basket he was using to cart things upstairs. *But it's the Patriots who are doing this to Francis.*

He climbed the stairs with heavy feet, leaving the empty shelves behind him. It was all so mixed up.

Thomas was halfway through wrapping the bottles and jars in newspaper and tying the packages with twine when he thought of something he was going to have to do now. Sam needed to know what Xavier had said about Alexander.

"Hutchinson, are you having some battle with yourself over there?" Francis said.

Thomas wondered what Francis was talking about until the apothecary shooed him out of the shop around sunset.

"You go on home now. We'll finish this up tomorrow." Francis gave a heavy sigh. "I haven't the heart for any more of this today."

When Thomas arrived at the college, the boys were still in class. Thomas went to Sam's room to wait for him. This time there were no voices coming from inside.

He sat down on Sam's bed and looked around. It was a small room without much furniture, and it was cluttered with books, papers, and assorted dirty clothes.

Esther would be having one of her fits if she saw this, Thomas thought.

He picked up a heavy volume that lay on the floor.

"'Metaphysics,'" he read out loud. He wasn't even sure what that was.

He got up and wandered around the room, looking at more books with mysterious titles and papers crammed with ciphering that looked more like Greek than arithmetic. On one paper, there was someone else's writing across the top in swirls and curlicues.

"Put forth more effort, Mr. Hutchinson," it said. "And spend less time daydreaming."

Thomas stared. Sam, daydreaming? He'd always been a good student. Mama and Papa couldn't stop bragging about how smart he was.

With nothing else to look at, Thomas sank down on the lumpy bed again and noticed an object on the candle stand. It was the watch, the one Thomas envied every time Sam took it out of his pocket.

I wonder what my sixteenth birthday present is going to be, he thought. *I wish it were going to be this.*

He lay back on the bed and held the globe-shaped watch over his head. Its glass and gold sent shimmers spinning around the ceiling like a sparkling top. He could have lain there all day, watching the light play above him, if there hadn't been something bumpy under the pillow. He put the watch back on the stand and fumbled under the cushion.

"What on earth?" he said out loud.

It was a bundle, all tied up as if someone were going to snatch it up and go on a journey. Thomas listened. There wasn't a sound in the hall. For some reason he wasn't quite sure of, he untied the bundle and let the sides of the cloth fall away.

Neatly arranged in front of him were two changes of linen, a pair of stockings, a razor, a cake of soap, and a needle and thread.

Wherever this person is going, he won't be staying long, Thomas thought.

And then he sat straight up as if he'd been poked in the back. What other "person" could it be besides Sam? Why would someone else have his traveling bundle under Sam's pillow?

The answer shot into his head like an arrow. Of course. Alexander.

✢ ⊹ ✢

Chapter Nine

Thomas stared down at the unfolded bundle. When it was time, Alexander was going to leave from here, and Sam was going to help him. Alexander wasn't fooling about going away to be a spy.

But for which side?

That thought had barely occurred to him when laughter began to fill the stairwell at the end of the hall. Sam's shout of a laugh shot above the others, and Thomas leaped from the bed, dropping the soap and razor on the floor.

He swallowed a cry and scooped them up. His hands shook as he stuffed them into the bundle with the linen and tied it back up. He was just cramming it under the pillow when Sam's voice rose outside the door.

"I'll see you at supper, then!" he called to someone. "Pray they have something we can actually eat, eh?"

Pray I don't look too guilty when he comes in, Thomas

thought. But he didn't pray. He just tried to look innocent.

The door swung open, and Sam flew in, robe dangling around him. He tossed his books on the floor with the others and only then saw Thomas sitting there.

"Little brother!" he said. "Welcome! What brings you here . . . besides the pleasure of my company?"

Thomas breathed a sigh of relief. Sam hadn't stopped grinning since he'd come in the door. He couldn't suspect that his "little brother" had been snooping under his pillow.

"I heard something today," Thomas said. "I thought you should know."

"Ah," Sam said. "So it *isn't* for the pleasure of my company. Oh, well." He pulled off his robe and straddled his desk chair. "What have you heard?"

"It's about Alexander."

Thomas watched Sam closely. His brother sat up straighter and watched him back, his smile fading.

"Go on," Sam said, in a very different voice.

Thomas spilled out the story of Xavier in the apothecary shop. When he was finished, Sam rested his chin on his hands on the back of the chair and was quiet for a long time. Thomas took that chance to glance at the pillow to make sure the bundle was all the way back in place. It was.

"Does Alexander have any reason not to trust you?" Sam asked suddenly.

Thomas shook his head.

"Good. Will you do something for me?"

"What?" Thomas said.

"If Alexander says or does anything that would make you

think that he is not, indeed, a Patriot, you must run here and tell me at once. Will you do that?"

Thomas frowned. "You don't think what Xavier said is true, do you?"

"Not a word of it! But if I'm going to—"

He stopped, and Thomas waited. Sam got up and wandered to the window where he stood staring out.

If you're going to what? Thomas wanted to say. He folded his arms and looked impatiently at the floor. His eyes lit on a cake of soap—the soap that had been in the bundle.

Oh, no! he thought wildly. *I thought I got it back in! I must have dropped it again!*

Heart pounding, Thomas looked up at Sam. He was still struggling with himself in front of the window. Leaning over stealthily, Thomas reached for the cake of soap. Just as his fingers curled around it, Sam turned around. Thomas put his hand in his lap, the soap folded in it, and looked innocently at his brother. Sam didn't seem to notice. His eyes didn't even meet Thomas's.

"I just have to be sure of Alexander," he said. "It's my duty as a Patriot."

"I'll do it," Thomas said quickly. He tried to keep himself from looking down into his lap. He could swear the soap was burning a hole in his palm. "I'll tell you anything I hear."

Sam flashed a smile. "Good boy," he said—and reached down a hand.

Thomas stared at it while his mind spun. *He wants to*

shake my hand. I can't let him see the soap! How am I going to—?

And then as if by magic, there was a knock on the door. Sam turned to open it, and Thomas stuck the soap inside his shirt, under his vest. There was no time to get it back into the bundle, but maybe Sam wouldn't look in it before Alexander took it away.

"I'll join you there," Sam said to the boy in the doorway. When he'd hurried off, Sam turned to Thomas. "Remember now," he whispered, "not a word of this to anyone."

"Not a word," Thomas said.

That's one more secret I have to keep, he thought as he hurried home by the glow of candlelit windows, with the cake of soap bouncing against his chest. *How am I going to be around Caroline and keep all of this from her? And how are we going to find Patsy's family if I'm not around her?*

He sighed and started up the front steps. Suddenly, something firm took hold of his ankle.

"What—?" Thomas cried out. But something else grabbed his other ankle, and he felt himself falling off the steps and into the bushes. His crash was broken by a pair of wiry arms.

"Malcolm!" Thomas said.

"Shhh! Your mama is right there in the dining room—and Esther, too." Malcolm was whispering so close to his ear that Thomas could feel his hot breath.

"Were you trying to break my legs?" Thomas whispered back.

"Those logs? Not a chance!"

Thomas peered at him through the darkness to see if the glint in Malcolm's sharp black eyes was from teasing—or anger. It looked like a little of both.

"Why did you do that?" Thomas hissed.

"I want to talk to you."

"Why did you have to take me down like I was a sheep you were about to shear?"

There was a short pause before Malcolm said, "The man of the house doesn't lower himself to come out to the kitchen or the stable anymore."

"And have you fire musket balls at me with your eyes? No, thank you."

Just then, the front door opened, and Malcolm clasped his hand over Thomas's mouth from behind.

"Who's out there?" Esther demanded.

Malcolm squeezed in, and Thomas nodded. It wouldn't do for either of them to be caught hiding. Esther didn't play games with servants or the children in her charge.

"What is it, Esther?" Mama called out anxiously from inside.

"Don't worry, Mistress Virginia," Esther said. "It isn't Tarleton's raiders. Not this time."

But through the leaves, Thomas could see her sweep the Palace Green once more with her eyes, and it occurred to him that she would be quite a match for the green-coated dragoons. Seemingly satisfied that she had made the street safe for her mistress, she ducked her head back inside and closed the door. Malcolm let go of Thomas's head.

"We'd better talk somewhere else," Malcolm whispered. "The stable. That is, if you don't think you'll get dirty there, sir."

Thomas bristled, but he followed Malcolm across the yard and behind the house where they crept past the chicken coops, the smokehouse, and the outdoor toilets on their way to the stable. Malcolm led Thomas to an empty stall and motioned for him to crouch down in the straw beside him.

"What is it?" Thomas asked. The back of his neck was still prickling.

"I know you've been lookin' for some clue to where Patsy's come from, and I need to ask you, have you found out anythin'?"

"I thought you said you could do it all by yourself. Why are you asking me?"

"Fine, then. Don't tell me."

Malcolm started to get up, but Thomas said quickly, "Wait. We haven't found out anything. Have you?"

"No, and I don't think we will, any of us."

We could if we worked as the Fearsome Trio, Thomas thought wistfully. Squatting here in the hay, talking to Malcolm, was like times not so long ago when he'd gone to Malcolm and Caroline with everything. He longed to tell Malcolm about Alexander . . . and about the bundle he'd found in Sam's room . . . and about what Xavier had done to Francis that day. But he'd made so many promises. It was like having a burden on his back, and he was beginning to hate it.

"I'm thinkin' we should give it up altogether," Malcolm said suddenly.

Thomas stared. "You mean, stop looking for her parents?"

"Why not? They certainly haven't come lookin' for her. What kind of mother and father are they anyway if they won't even watch over a little girl who can't speak?"

"But what will happen to her if we can't find them?" Thomas asked.

"Perhaps Peggy Cheswell would take her in," Malcolm said. "She has no one to help her."

Thomas wrinkled his nose. "Who would want to live with that whining old woman?"

"You would if you had no place else to go!" Malcolm cried.

"But how do we know Patsy doesn't?"

Malcolm looked hard at him and then stood up to look down at Thomas. "Never you mind, sir," he said, his thin upper lip curled. "What do you care if someone is all alone in the world? You don't know what that's like and you never will, so what is it to you? I never should have troubled myself trying to talk to you."

With that, Malcolm stalked across the hay-strewn floor and out of the stable. Thomas stared out the doorway long after he was gone.

I think I do know what it's like to be all alone, he thought sadly. *I've never felt so alone in my life. Do I really have to carry all this by myself?*

He went up to his room with an aching longing for Papa in his chest.

The following Sunday was one of those brilliant fall days in Williamsburg that carried with it both the sunshiny glow of the summer gone by and the crisp hint of the sparkling winter to come. As Mama, Esther, Otis, Malcolm, and Thomas walked to Bruton Parish Church, the catalpa trees along the Palace Green dangled their seed pods playfully overhead and the bobwhite quail whistled back and forth as if they had a game in progress.

But it all made Thomas even sadder. This was the kind of Sunday when he, Malcolm, and Caroline used to slip away and find some magnificent imaginary adventure to play out amid the blur of colorful trees and piles of fallen leaves.

There are no imaginary adventures anymore, he thought solemnly as he trailed behind the others. *Everything is too real. There are too many burdens.*

The Hutchinsons, Mama and Thomas, went to their usual pew in the main part of the church, while Malcolm, Otis, and Esther sat with the other servants in the left gallery. Thomas knew the seats there didn't have cushions on them like his did. But he was convinced they couldn't have been any more uncomfortable. The backs of the seats went straight up, so that everyone had to sit like a ramrod throughout the very long service.

Thomas had actually come to love Bruton Parish Church— the white, airy walls, the curved windows, and the pulpit raised high above them where the kind Reverend Pendleton preached his sermons. Thomas liked how the whole building was shaped like a cross and how at the top of it, behind the altar, were the tablets containing the Ten Commandments, the Lord's Prayer, and the Apostles' Creed. He'd learned them all from studying with Alexander and listening at Evening Prayer when Papa was with them.

The service, which they all followed in the *Book of Common Prayer,* had a lot of big words that Alexander still hadn't taught him. But he'd had some important moments in this church, and it was usually a good thing to be here.

But today Thomas's mind was so troubled that he couldn't think or feel anything good. Every time he looked up into the left gallery, he caught Malcolm glaring at him. Whenever he looked over at Caroline across the aisle with her parents and Alexander, his thoughts became more tangled than a ball of Esther's yarn.

It's too much, he thought angrily. *I shouldn't have so many hard things to think about!*

He was about to settle in and think about something else—like whether Betsy Taylor was going to send over more apple tarts today—when Reverend Edmond Pendleton's voice brushed that aside like a hand clearing a table.

"'Bear ye one another's burdens,'" he was saying. "St. Paul's letter to the Galatians, chapter six. 'Bear ye one another's burdens, and so fulfill the law of Christ.'"

As the reverend looked down over the congregation, Thomas caught his breath.

Is he looking at me? Thomas thought. *Is he talking right to me?*

"In this time of war and mistrust and fear," Reverend Pendleton went on, "we all have a responsibility to God to help each other lighten our loads. Not one of us can be content unless all of us are fed and clothed and safe from danger. We must bear not only our own burdens, but those of our brothers and sisters as well."

For an instant, Thomas was sure the reverend's eyes locked with his. He was almost sure that the minister added, "Do you hear that, Thomas Hutchinson?"

"Yes, sir," Thomas whispered.

Mama looked down at him curiously.

Maybe I shouldn't have so many things to think about and so many secrets to keep, Thomas thought, *but I do.*

And it was certain now that he was going to have to bear them all. Alone.

✠ ✠ ✠

homas was walking home from church that day as if he truly had several packs on his back when a familiar rickety wagon and a bony old horse pulled up beside the Hutchinson group. Dr. Nicholas Quincy shined his shy smile at them from the driver's seat.

"Good day," he said, "and a happy Sabbath to you."

Nicholas was a Quaker and didn't attend Bruton Parish Church, which was Church of England. But Thomas could see from the doctor's best black coat and starched white shirt that he had been to his own meeting.

"Good day, Nicholas!" Mama called back to him in her song of a voice. "How lovely to see you! Will you join us for Sunday dinner?"

A pink patch appeared on each of Nicholas's cheeks. "That's nice of you, Mistress Hutchinson, but I had something else in mind."

He's tasted Esther's cooking! Thomas told himself. He wanted to share that thought with Malcolm, but the servant boy was drawing in the dust with his toe.

"I wondered if I might steal Thomas and Malcolm away for the afternoon," Dr. Quincy said to Mama. "Our little Patsy is well enough to hobble about on that foot, and she needs some fresh air and the company of other children. I thought to take them all on an outing—Caroline, too."

"How wonderful!" Mama said. "I'll have Esther prepare a picnic lunch."

"Oh, there's no need," Nicholas said. "Mistress Taylor has already volunteered her cook."

Thomas thanked heaven for that—and for the fact that Mama immediately gave her consent. As soon as Malcolm and Thomas had changed their clothes, they climbed into the wagon waiting in front of the house and looked at each other warily. Caroline was already perched on a bench in back. Beside her sat Patsy, who had eyes only for Malcolm.

Thomas looked carefully at her as he hoisted himself into the wagon and sat on the other side of her. Her black braids fell from under a three-cornered scarf tied under her chin. It made her face look like a happy little triangle, with two huge eyes staring out of it. He had never seen her out and about like one of them, and he was surprised at how wiry and strong she looked, even in her faded flowered dress with the ragged lace at the elbows. He noticed that it was shabby, compared to Caroline's makeover with its petticoat that peeked out from the bottom and the long sleeves with the ruffles at the wrists.

"That's probably an old dress of the Widow Cheswell's that she made over for her," Caroline whispered to him later. "Peggy could have done better than that for her, but don't stare at her so."

That really wasn't why he was staring; it was more because of how very normal Patsy looked now. And how taken she was by Malcolm. That part was almost embarrassing, as far as Thomas was concerned.

As the wagon, pulled by old Dolly, bounced along the road toward the James River, Patsy followed Malcolm's face with her eyes and almost mouthed his every word with her own lips. When he smiled, she smiled. When he laughed, she threw her head back, too, though she didn't make a sound.

And when Malcolm scowled across the wagon at Thomas, Patsy frowned at him, too.

I haven't done anything to you! Thomas wanted to shout at her. *I'm trying to find your family for you!*

Caroline didn't seem to notice any of that. She was too busy pointing out all the sights to Patsy, giggling at Malcolm's jokes, and asking Nicholas how much longer it would be before they got there.

"Stop here, Dr. Quincy!" she would call out every few minutes. "I like this spot!"

But Nicholas drove on until they found a place worth waiting for. The sun streamed through the canopy of color created by the trees and sparkled on the water just beyond them. Caroline agreed that it was indeed perfect.

A quilt was spread out and on it, Caroline and Patsy displayed the banquet the Taylors' cook had packed in the basket. Thomas felt his mouth watering.

There was boiled ham and goose and some turkey, too, as well as pigeon pie, bread and jelly, and dessert of plums, almonds, and apples. Thomas had second helpings of everything, but that didn't keep him from noticing that Patsy was almost keeping up with him.

"I've never seen you eat so much!" Caroline said to her. She turned to Dr. Quincy. "Does that mean she's getting better?"

"I would say that within a few weeks, she'll be walking on her own again, without having to hold on to anyone."

Without having to hold on to Malcolm, you mean, Thomas thought.

"Did you hear that, Patsy?" Caroline said.

Malcolm frowned at her, his black eyebrows knitted together. "Of course she heard it. She isn't *deaf!*"

"How do you know?" Caroline said. "She can't talk, after all."

"Malcolm is right," Dr. Quincy said, helping himself to a handful of almonds. "I have examined Patsy carefully, and I can find no physical reason why she doesn't talk."

Caroline polished an apple on her skirt. "So she can talk, but she won't. Why is that?"

"Maybe she just doesn't have anything to say," Malcolm said sharply.

"Right again," said Nicholas. "And perhaps we should all keep our mouths closed more often, eh?"

Caroline laughed. "I don't think I'll ever do that!"

That's what I'm doing, though, Thomas thought. *I'm keeping my mouth shut about Alexander and about the army taking all of Francis's medicine. If Nicholas says so, then it must be right.*

"Penny for your thoughts, Tom," Caroline said.

"I'm keeping my mouth shut," he said.

With lunch over, the afternoon stretched before them like a long, inviting road. Nicholas wandered a little ways off to investigate the plant life, and Caroline said, "What shall we play?"

"Captain John Smith," said Thomas.

Malcolm made a sour face. "I'm tired of that. We play that every time we come here."

"But we always have fun at it," Caroline said.

Malcolm gave Thomas a dark look and shrugged. Thomas felt as if he'd been slapped.

"I'll just sit here with Patsy, since she can't play anyway," Malcolm said.

Caroline put her hands on her hips. "Why not? She isn't made of glass, Malcolm. She just has a hurt foot."

"How will she get around?" Malcolm asked.

Caroline looked thoughtful for a moment and then threw up her hands as if the answer had been dangling in front of them all the time. "Tom can haul her on his back! We'll pretend she's the damsel in distress and you're a dragon about to eat her, when Thomas comes to the rescue and carries her away."

"I carry her?"

"Why does *he* carry her?"

Malcolm and Thomas blurted out their questions at the same time, and Caroline narrowed her eyes at them.

"What is going on between you two?" she asked.

There was a stony silence. Caroline tossed her head and turned to Patsy.

"All right, then," she said. "You and I will just have to play by ourselves, since all these two can do is fight."

"Let him do it," Thomas said quickly. "If he's going to sulk about it, I'll be the dragon. Where is my cave?"

Caroline, of course, had it all figured out. Holding on to Caroline's arm, Patsy hobbled to a spot close to the river where an overgrowth of bushes formed a hideaway, the closest thing to a cave they could find. Patsy was settled in, with Thomas lurking and slavering about, and Malcolm was sent out into the forest to start his quest.

"Who are you going to be?" Thomas asked Caroline.

"I'm your assistant dragon," she said promptly. "We're always partners, Tom," she added in a whisper.

Thomas felt a pang he was pretty sure was guilt. Partners didn't usually keep secrets from each other. But he'd promised Sam. And if she knew the truth about Alexander, she wouldn't be smiling and flashing her dimples the way she was right now.

"All right, then," he said to her. "I think I smell a lousy knight, searching for the fair maiden."

It was a marvelous crusade, and Thomas the Tireless Dragon was just about to roar mightily at Malcolm the Mighty when a crack split the air.

Everyone froze. It was a sound they knew well by now.

"That was gunfire!" Malcolm said.

In one leap he was in the "cave," pushing Patsy to the

ground and covering her with his body like a human shield. Before Thomas could even move, Nicholas was behind him, pushing him with one hand and Caroline with the other. He flattened them both under him as the shots continued to pop and snap.

Thomas had never felt his heart slam harder against the inside of his chest. His thoughts ran wild. *Is it the British? Have Tarleton's dragoons come to raid Williamsburg? Will they shoot us because we're Patriots?*

"Dr. Quincy?" Malcolm whispered. "Listen to the rhythm of those shots. It sounds like target practice."

Thomas felt Nicholas stiffen to listen. Then he rolled off Thomas and Caroline and, putting his finger to his lips, nodded at Malcolm. His already pale face was ghost-white and taut as a bowstring, but he took a deep breath and raised his shoulders slowly above the bushes.

"You there!" he called out. "You, sir, with the gun! Hold your fire! There are children here!"

Another shot barked across the afternoon, and Thomas squeezed his eyes shut. Beside him, he heard Caroline whimper.

"Hold your fire, sir!" Nicholas shouted again. "We have children here!"

They waited, but the woods were still. Then they heard the crunch of footsteps across the carpet of pine needles.

"Stay down!" Nicholas whispered hoarsely.

He himself continued to stand with his head sticking out of the "cave."

"Please get down, sir!" Thomas whispered.

But another voice drowned his out.

"Hallo, there!" it cried. "Who's there?"

"Dr. Nicholas Quincy!"

There were more footsteps, and a shaken voice said, "I beg your pardon. I didn't know there was anyone here. Truly I didn't."

"Would you put your gun down, sir?" Nicholas said.

"I was only practicin'! I'm going into the militia, you know."

"Fine, sir," Nicholas said. His gentle voice was growing firmer. "But just for safekeeping, would you mind putting the gun down for now? We want no accidents."

There was a pause, and then the sound of an object thudding to the ground. Thomas thought he heard Nicholas sigh.

"Dr. Quincy, you say?" the man said. His voice still trembled—like a bad boy who has been caught at mischief, Thomas thought.

"Yes. And who might you be?"

"My name is Clark," the man answered. "Walter Clark."

✢ ✢ ✢

Chapter Eleven

Thomas didn't wait for Nicholas to give him permission to stand and neither did Caroline. They both popped up from the bushes and stared.

The man who stared back at them with bewildered, painful-looking blue eyes was the same man who had tried to steal a gun from George Fenton's shop. It was Walter Clark indeed.

"I didn't know there was anyone here. Truly I didn't," he said again. He was shaking his tousled reddish head much harder than he had to. He looked as if they all had him in a corner.

"It's quite all right, Mr. Clark," Nicholas said. "There was no harm done."

"But I had to practice, you see, because I'm going off to the war," Walter said, as if Nicholas hadn't spoken a word. "I'm going to join the militia."

He kept babbling on to Nicholas about fighting for the Patriot cause and having to practice. He said that again and again until Thomas got a queasy feeling in his stomach.

Caroline tugged at Thomas's sleeve and put her mouth close to his ear.

"So he got a gun after all," she whispered.

Thomas nodded.

"That's a Brown Bess you have there," Malcolm said from behind them.

Thomas tried not to roll his eyes. *He's showing off again,* he thought.

"Not a very accurate weapon," Malcolm went on, "but it will do for standin' shoulder to shoulder in the infantry and firin' into a whole company."

"Oh, that's not the kind of shooting I'm going to be doing!" Walter cried. He shook his head just as vigorously as he'd nodded it before. Caroline grabbed Thomas's sleeve again and pulled him a few steps backward.

"I'm going to fight with Francis Marion in South Carolina or go down and help ward off old Tarleton!" Walter said. His ruddy face grew redder, and his hair seemed to stand straight up on end. Thomas could see him swallowing hard. "No sissy fighting for me, no sir! I want to go where the real action is!"

No one answered. There seemed to be nothing to say. Even Nicholas stood studying the man.

"You don't believe me!" Walter burst out suddenly. "You don't believe me! No one believes me! But I will. You just wait and see! I will!"

He looked frantically down at the gun, and in one horrible instant, Thomas knew he was going to grab for it. In that same instant, Dr. Quincy cut in front of him and firmly grabbed his shoulders, and Malcolm slid across the ground and snatched up the Brown Bess.

"We all believe you, Mr. Clark," Nicholas said softly. "There's not a one of us here who doesn't. You'll be a fine soldier, I'm sure."

"I'm not sure," Thomas muttered.

Caroline poked him.

"That's my gun!" Walter hollered at Malcolm.

He started to lunge toward him, arms flailing under Nicholas's grip.

"Whoa there, sir!" Nicholas cried. With a heave, he pulled Walter back. Malcolm tossed the gun far out of reach.

"My gun!" Walter shouted. "He's stealing my gun!"

"No one is stealing it," Nicholas said. His voice was still calm, but Thomas saw the muscles working in his cheeks. "We're just getting it out of the way so no one gets hurt, eh?"

"You can't take it from me."

"No, it's right there. When I let you go, I want you to pick it up and leave this place. Then no one will get hurt."

Walter seemed to be trying to get himself under control. He nodded, fast and hard at first, but gradually slowing down and steadying his eyes on the gun. Still, Nicholas motioned for the children to get down, and they did. Only Malcolm peeked above the bushes to watch.

"Is he gone?" Caroline whispered after a few moments.

"Yes, thank heaven!" Malcolm said. "That man's daft!"

Nicholas parted the bushes and said, "Come along, children. I think it's time we went home."

As he herded them toward the wagon, Thomas glanced over his shoulder. Walter Clark was long gone, and he'd taken his gun with him.

"I'd hate to see him with a gun, even if he could afford one," George Fenton had said about Walter. "All of Williamsburg would have to go into hiding."

Thomas decided he was right. And yet there was something so strange about the man—so sad—as if he just wanted to be important.

Malcolm went with Dr. Quincy to take Patsy back to the Widow Cheswell's house. Thomas and Caroline settled themselves in the oak tree behind Thomas's house, each with an apple left from the picnic.

"I don't think we should try to talk to Lydia Clark again," Thomas said. "Not after what happened today."

"She doesn't know anything anyway," Caroline said.

Thomas stopped in mid-bite. "How do you know?"

"Race you to the top of the tree, Tom!" she said suddenly. And tossing her apple core to the ground, she was up the trunk like a monkey.

Thomas shook his head and lumbered after her.

Sitting beside Thomas the next morning at lessons, Alexander said, "Hello? Thomas? Anyone at home?"

Thomas jerked his face up to meet Alexander's gaze. The

teacher looked as if he were waiting for the answer to some question, but Thomas had been busy thinking about what kind of spy Alexander really was.

"Did you say something?" Thomas said feebly.

"Several things, but I'll try to keep it simple." Alexander grinned at him. "What—did—you—read—in—the—newspaper—for—today?"

Thomas squirmed. "Well, sir—"

"Say no more," Alexander said. "When you start calling me sir, I know you didn't do it."

Thomas looked miserably at the tabletop. He'd really meant to, but there had been so much else to do and think about. He'd just forgotten, even after Caroline had reminded him.

"I'm going to quit this job and start teaching my sister," Alexander said with a gleam in his brown eyes. "At least she does the assignments."

Thomas felt his brow pucker.

"I've seen her every day," Alexander went on, "poring over the *Virginia Gazette* as if there were no tomorrow."

Thomas gulped. "I'll do it today. I promise!"

"You certainly will," Alexander said, "because I have one right here." He spread the newspaper on the table with one hand and patted it with the other. "Get to work!"

"All of it?"

"Front to back."

Thomas leaned his elbows on the table and scanned the front page. There was nothing there that he didn't know from listening to Papa at the supper table. Tarleton's raids.

Benedict Arnold turning traitor. The hospital for soldiers being set up in the Governor's Palace.

Thomas gave a grunt and turned the page. Advertisements ran up and down in strips. The first one read:

WANTED

Ran away from the subscriber, an indentured schoolteacher named Silas Lewis, about 24 years of age. He had on when he ran away a cloth jacket and dark trousers. He is five feet and four inches in height and of heavy build. All vessels and others are forbid harboring or carrying off said man.

   John Hart
   No. 2 South Second Street, Philadelphia

If Malcolm ran away, Thomas thought, *I would have to put an ad like that in the paper, since I'm in charge until Papa comes home.*

Thomas felt a tightness in his throat and quickly turned the page. Missing his good times with Malcolm was another burden he had to bear.

"Find anything interesting?" Alexander said.

"No," Thomas said glumly. "Let's do arithmetic."

Going to work at the apothecary shop that afternoon didn't cheer him up. Francis's face was as long as an afternoon shadow when Thomas came in.

Instead of "hello," the old man said, "I took most of the

items Wormeley wanted over to the Governor's Palace, but there are a few things left." He snapped his head toward a pair of large bundles on the counter. "Deliver them, would you?"

Thomas looked at him curiously. The old apothecary's shoulders were sagging, and he reminded Thomas of a worn-out bird. As ancient as he was, he'd never looked like this before.

"Yes, sir," Thomas said.

It was a drizzly afternoon, and the mud on the Palace Green sucked at the soles of Thomas's shoes as he mucked his way to the Governor's Palace. The catalpa trees were drooping with the rain, just the way Thomas's spirits were wilting.

Even the Palace looked gloomy as he stopped in front of it. He remembered that when he was a little boy this build-ing was the most magnificent in Williamsburg, maybe even in all of Virginia. Now the tall wrought iron gate that framed the entrance was rusted and chipped, and so many rocks had been thrown at the emblem on the top that it was dented and in danger of falling off completely. Thomas knew the letters on it—GR—stood for "George Rex," the King of England. Sam always said he wished he'd been here when they'd done that; he would have joined them. He wondered if Alexander thought that now, too. Thomas went on through the gate, trying not to remember all the fun he and Caroline and Malcolm had had here.

He crept nervously through the ballroom doorway and tripped on a piece of brick that had fallen from the bracket of carved bricks above his head. He stumbled into the hall and had to grab for the wall to keep from sprawling on the floor and taking the packages with him. When he pulled back his hand, it was covered with crumbled blue wallpaper. He was standing, staring at it, when a man in a blue-and-scarlet uniform strode up to him.

"What are you about here, boy?" he said. His voice wasn't stern, but it was full of business. Thomas straightened and wiped his hand on the back of his breeches.

"I've come with the rest of the medicine from the apothecary's." Thomas tried to sound angry and disapproving, but it was hard with this officer looking down at him out of busy eyes. Everything about him, in fact, was busy, and with good reason. Behind him, the once-elegant ballroom was bustling with men scrubbing the floors with brushes and rolling out blankets along the walls.

"We already received several large bundles last week," the officer said. "This is more?"

Thomas puffed out his chest. "Francis Pickering is the finest apothecary in all of Virginia," he said. "He had every medicine you can name, and the soldiers are to have it all."

"This Mr. Pickering must be a fine Patriot as well, then," the officer said. "Please extend our thanks to him. He is truly dedicated to the cause."

He doesn't have much choice, Thomas wanted to say. But he only nodded and backed away.

The officer's eyes sprang open, and he cried, "Watch—"

But it was too late. Thomas had already backed into a glass-fronted cabinet that stood in the middle of the room.

He turned in time to see it sway perilously, rocking the jars and bottles and syrup pots inside. The officer lunged for it and steadied it just before it toppled over. Thomas could only stare at it—because it held all of Francis's precious medicines.

"Sorry," Thomas said abruptly. And he ran out the way he'd come in.

He tried to go back to the apothecary shop, but the thought of facing Francis and telling him that he'd seen his life's work standing idle was more of a burden than even he could carry. He decided to take the long way back.

He slowed down at the corner of Francis and Blair to shake the water off his hat when he heard voices—loud voices—coming from the gunsmith's shop.

"This is as bad as robbery, George Fenton, and you know it!" shouted one voice. "These prices are ridiculous!"

"Then take your business elsewhere!" shouted the other. "I don't need your insults, Alexander Taylor!"

✥ ✥ ✥

Chapter Twelve

homas stood gaping at the slightly open front door of the shop. His mind was in a tumble. *Alexander! In the gunsmith's?*

"I am presenting facts, Mr. Fenton!" Alexander shouted now. "If they are insulting to you, I'm sorry!"

Thomas had never heard Alexander sound this way. His voice could be full of mischief or fun or even fire, but never anger. Thomas didn't want to hear it, and he turned to race back through the rain to the apothecary shop.

But he'd taken only a few steps when he remembered what Sam had said: "If Alexander says or does anything that would make you think he is not indeed a Patriot, you must run here and tell me at once."

Thomas stopped and inched closer to the shop. *Could this be it?* he thought frantically. *It sounds like Alexander is trying to buy a gun. Is it for the Patriots—or because he's a Loyalist spy?* He chewed at the inside of his mouth. *I promised Sam. I have to find out.*

With a sense of dread heavier than any of his burdens, Thomas took the final steps to the gunsmith's front walk and slid under a dripping maple to listen.

There had been a long pause, and now George Fenton filled it with a voice he was obviously trying to control.

"I've always liked you, Alexander," he said. "I've found you to be a reasonable young man. So will you please listen?"

"I won't listen to excuses, George," Alexander said. His voice, too, was quieter, but it was still tinged with impatience.

"I had to raise my prices—again," George Fenton said. "Or I'd starve to death."

Alexander grunted. "Nonsense. Everyone in town seems to be buying a gun these days, what with rumors of Tarleton coming closer. You ought to be lowering your prices with all that business."

"I would—if people weren't coming in here and stealing them right out from under my nose!"

"Stealing?" Alexander said. "My sister said Walter Clark tried to steal one from you, but he didn't get away with it."

"Not that day," said George. "But he, or someone else, managed to take one just this last Saturday. Look there— see those empty pegs?"

Thomas could imagine George waving an arm up at the wall where there should have been a gun but wasn't. Thomas wondered if the vacant space had once held a Brown Bess.

He heard Alexander give another grunt. *"One* gun was

stolen so you've doubled the price of every other weapon in the place?"

"I have to feed my family, same as your father. I don't complain about the price of milling grain!"

"That's because my father isn't trying to take everything you own to pay for it!" Alexander cried. "Good day, Mr. Fenton!"

Thomas tried to scramble out of his hiding place so he wouldn't look like he'd been spying. But Alexander was out the door and down the steps before Thomas could peel the wet leaves off his sleeves. His teacher stopped on the walkway, and Thomas could see him trying to squeeze the anger out of his face.

"If you're going in there to buy a gun, Thomas," he said, "don't bother. The man's a money-grubbing merchant, and that's all!"

Thomas hurried to fall into step with Alexander, who was wasting no time in putting distance between himself and the gunsmith's shop.

"I don't need a gun," Thomas said as he tripped along beside him. "But why do you?"

Alexander kept walking with his hands behind his back, honey-blond head bent against the rain, and for a few moments Thomas wasn't sure he was going to answer. But he suddenly took Thomas by the sleeve and pulled him into the shelter of the old Capitol Building. Without stopping to shake the water from his clothes, he leaned close to Thomas and said, "Can you keep a secret, young Hutchinson?"

Thomas nearly groaned out loud. *Another one?* he

wanted to cry. *I can barely walk because of the weight of these secrets as it is!*

But he nodded and listened.

"I have a friend," Alexander half-whispered, "who wants to join a company of the army that is very far away from here. He will need a gun to join, and for certain reasons I can't share with you, he can't obtain a weapon on his own. I've offered to help him." He glanced away from Thomas and stared off over his head at the rain.

Thomas's mind spun like a top. He wasn't sure what some of those words meant, but from the way Alexander refused to look at him, he did know one thing: Some of what Alexander was saying was a lie.

"You must trust me that it is important for this to remain a secret," Alexander said. "You do trust me, don't you, young Hutchinson?"

Thomas closed his eyes. *No!* he almost cried out. *I used to! You were the one who convinced me I was smart! You were the one who understood whenever I was confused! You told me you would never wish the Patriots any harm! But you're lying to me now!*

He opened his eyes to find Alexander studying his face the way he had so many times before when he was waiting for an answer. His brown eyes looked honest again, and Thomas couldn't say any of the things he was thinking.

"What is it, Thomas?" Alexander said. "You look confused. How can I help you?"

"I *am* confused," Thomas said.

Alexander nodded in his understanding way, and Thomas

almost told him everything . . . that he knew he was claiming to be a Patriot . . . that Sam wasn't sure he could trust him. . . .

And then he thought of Sam again—Sam saying he had to be sure of Alexander, if he were going to . . . going to what?

Sam had never said what it was he was going to do, but suddenly it was as clear to Thomas as the drops that hit his face.

Alexander was trying to buy a gun for Sam. It's Sam who's going away to fight in the war. It was Sam's own bundle he had hidden under his pillow. Sam had to be sure he could trust Alexander if he was going to help Sam run away.

With a pang that went all the way through him, Thomas shook his head at Alexander. "I'll figure it out," he said. "I don't need any help."

Alexander looked deep into him, and Thomas couldn't stand it any longer. Without even saying good-bye, he took off across the soggy Capitol lawn.

Alexander didn't call to him.

Thomas went down to the cellar as soon as he got back to the apothecary shop. Except for the herbs hanging from the ceiling, it was empty now—just as Thomas was inside.

There were certainly no answers in there. Only questions.

Is Alexander going to help Sam—or hurt him?

If he's trying to help Sam, why didn't he tell me? Why wouldn't he look me in the eye?

I'm supposed to tell Sam anything I know, but what do I know?

Is Sam really going to run away and do something Papa has forbidden him to do?

Why can't Papa be here so I can tell him?

What can I do?

"Hutchinson! Is that you?" said a creaky old voice from above.

"Yes, sir," Thomas said.

The steps squeaked, and Francis joined him in the damp darkness. His usual skittering bird walk had slowed almost to a crawl, and he sighed heavily as he looked around at the naked shelves and cabinets.

"You made that delivery, did you?" he said.

Thomas nodded.

There was a long silence while Francis continued to stare at the empty shelves. It made Thomas's heart sink.

"Shall I grind some ginger for cough syrup, sir?" he asked.

Francis looked up at the dried herbs hanging from the ceiling, but he shook his head. "Perhaps tomorrow, eh? You run on home now."

Thomas felt his face wrinkle into a question mark that stayed there even after old Francis had made his way slowly up the stairs. Once again the question hammered in his head: *I thought the Patriot cause was supposed to be a good thing.*

It was still early afternoon, and Thomas didn't want to go home. Malcolm would be working, and besides, he wasn't even speaking to Thomas anymore. Caroline would be with her mother, practicing her needlework and the other "female arts" she was always complaining about. He could try to find Sam, but what would he say to him? *Are you really going to run away from home and join the army?*

But he didn't want to be by himself right now, and his lonely footsteps kept taking him farther from the Palace Green and the Hutchinsons' house. He was practically in front of Peggy Cheswell's when he realized he was going to see Patsy.

"Am I glad to see you!" the old widow said when she opened the front door to Thomas.

He looked over his shoulder to be sure she was talking to him.

"That girl's been restless as a cat in a room full of rocking chairs today!" Mistress Cheswell whined. She impatiently brushed back a wisp of her thin hair. "She keeps going to the window and looking out and sighing as if I were keeping her locked up here. Go on up there and entertain her, will you?"

Thomas nodded and headed for the staircase. He could still hear the old lady muttering below when he got to the top of the stairs: "Give the child a place to live until they find her parents, and she acts like I'm keeping her prisoner."

Thomas looked around the hall before he went to Patsy's room. Peggy Cheswell's house wasn't quite as bad as the jail, but if you couldn't come and go, it might seem a little like a prison. It was dark, musty, and deadly silent.

I'd rather hear Esther rattling on than listen to that, Thomas thought.

When he pushed open Patsy's door, she was standing at

the window. She looked back at him with a two-dimpled smile that disappeared as soon as she saw that he wasn't Malcolm. But that was all right with Thomas. He didn't want her hanging on him the way she did Malcolm. In fact, at this moment, he wasn't even sure why he'd come.

"Hello," he said, for lack of anything else to say.

She didn't answer, of course.

"I'm sorry I'm not Malcolm," he said, poking at the rug with his toe. "He's still working, you know—he practically runs our place for my father—now that Esther and Otis are so old and I'm so busy with school and working for Mr. Pickering—you know, the apothecary—Malcolm will probably come to see you later—but I thought you might be lonely now."

Thomas took a huge breath and felt his face start to burn. He knew he was rambling on, but it was hard to talk to someone who didn't answer. Right now, Patsy was just looking at him, blinking her big, sad eyes.

I thought Caroline had the biggest eyes in the world, Thomas thought. *But hers have never looked this sad.*

"Well, I suppose I ought to go now, and you can wait for Malcolm," Thomas said.

But as he turned to leave, he heard a whimper behind him. He looked at her quickly. She had hobbled a few steps toward him, and she was shaking her head vigorously.

Thomas swallowed. "You don't want me to go?"

She kept shaking her head.

"Then what shall we do?"

Patsy pointed to the window.

"Do you think Mistress Cheswell will let you go outside with me?" he said.

Her two dimples reappeared, and she nodded eagerly.

Thomas barely got the question out before Peggy Cheswell was agreeing to let Patsy go anywhere she wanted with Thomas—and stay as long as she liked. But when they got to the front door, Thomas looked at the little girl doubtfully.

"You still can't walk very far on your foot, can you?" he asked.

She shook her head, and then her face lit up. Taking him by the shoulders, she turned him around and patted his back.

"You want to ride on my back?"

Patsy nodded.

I'm going to walk around Williamsburg carrying a girl? Thomas thought in a panic. *What if someone sees me?*

But Patsy took his silence for a "yes" and hoisted herself up on his back with her arms around his neck. Peggy Cheswell hurried to open the door, and Thomas was suddenly out in the newly washed world with a girl clinging to him like a piece of ivy.

I have to get out of here before somebody spots us! he thought wildly. He took off like a shot down Francis Street.

✝ ⋅✝⋅ ✝

Chapter Thirteen

"Where shall we go?" he said to Patsy over his shoulder. It had stopped raining, and the fresh air made him feel frisky. Thomas looked around. They were across the street from the Clarks' house.

We surely don't want to go there, he thought.

But the idea had barely crossed his mind when the front door of the run-down little house opened and a bony young woman stepped out and looked at the day as if she'd been in the dark for a long time. She folded her arms across her chest and blinked.

"That must be Lydia Clark," Thomas said to Patsy in a low voice. "I've seen her before, but only with her face barely peeking out the door."

He took a good look at her now. She couldn't have been much older than his brother Clayton, about 19. Her mouse-brown hair was pulled straight back into a collection of thin ringlets at the base of her neck and, standing there rubbing her arms and licking her lips, she looked fragile, as people do when they are just getting over being sick.

Just then, Lydia caught sight of them and to Thomas's surprise, she waved and made her way around the puddles to cross the street.

"Hello there," she said. She offered a tiny smile that matched the rest of her very small features.

Thomas didn't know what else to do but nod.

"You are the boy who came by the other day, aren't you?" she asked in a timid voice.

Thomas nodded again.

Lydia put her almost-transparent hand up to her lips as if she were embarrassed. "I'm sorry I couldn't talk then. My husband has told me to be careful about strangers."

"Oh," Thomas said.

There was an awkward silence. Thomas wished she would go back into her house—before Walter stormed out waving his Brown Bess.

But Lydia made no move to go anywhere. She nodded toward Patsy. "Who is this you're carrying?" she asked.

"Patsy," Thomas said, glancing nervously toward the house.

"Patsy who?"

"We don't know, and she won't tell us. We . . . we found her."

"Hello there!" Lydia said. Up until now, her face had looked more than pale; it was colorless. But as she smiled at Patsy, her cheeks blushed pink, and her tiny hazel eyes lit up like little candle flames. She held out her hand, and to Thomas's amazement, Patsy put hers timidly in it.

"May she get down?" Lydia said.

Before Thomas could explain that Patsy had a hurt foot, the little girl scrambled off his back and stood on one leg, smiling up at Lydia.

"You're such a pretty little girl!" Lydia said. "How old are you?"

Patsy promptly held up 10 fingers. Thomas stared at her.

"You're 10?" he said.

At once, Patsy tucked both hands behind her back and looked a little frightened, but Lydia laughed softly.

"You're just dainty," she said to Patsy. "Not everyone is a big, strapping boy like he is, eh?"

Patsy smiled again and nodded. Lydia went on to comment about her dress and her shiny braids and other girl things while Thomas watched in awe.

Is this the same Patsy? he thought. *And is this the same Lydia Clark? She looks so . . . so calm!*

Maybe she was calm enough to answer a question or two.

Thomas pretended to draw in the mud with his toe and said casually, "So your husband was finally able to buy a gun, eh?"

Lydia glanced at him and went back to retying Patsy's drooping hair ribbon.

"We saw him with it Sunday," Thomas went on. "He told us he was practicing to join the militia."

Lydia gave him her full attention then, and her smile faded as she looked both ways and leaned toward Thomas.

"He tried to join the militia last summer," she said in a whisper, "but they wouldn't take him. He isn't going into the army at all. I don't know why he bought that gun."

"He said he was buying it for you," Thomas said. "So you could protect yourself while he was gone. That's what he said that day in the gunsmith's shop when—"

He stopped. Maybe she didn't know her husband was going around trying to steal guns, and Thomas didn't want to tell her. She looked so brittle that she would probably break into pieces if he did.

She put a hand lightly on his arm. "Please, don't tell anyone what I told you. Walter wants to fight for the Patriots so badly. It shames him that he can't go."

Thomas was about to ask her why, when a raindrop hit his face, and then another.

"It's starting to rain again," he said. "I have to take Patsy home."

"Will you bring her back to see me?" Lydia said.

Thomas didn't have to answer. Patsy was bobbing her head up and down as she climbed onto Thomas's back. Lydia smiled her tiny smile.

Thomas was sorry to drop Patsy off at Peggy Cheswell's, and he would have taken her around the block a few more times, even in the rain, if she hadn't started to nod. She smiled sleepily as he deposited her on her bed. But when she reached up and touched his face, Thomas darted from the room like a cottontail, his face crimson.

Still, as he hurried out of the house, he had to admit

that Patsy was one burden he hadn't minded carrying. Not more than a little bit.

He was headed toward home when Nicholas's creaky wagon splashed up next to him and old Dolly nuzzled his elbow. Thomas grinned as he wrapped his arms around the horse's long neck.

"Where are you off to in the rain?" Nicholas called from the driver's seat.

"No place," Thomas said.

"Would you like to go 'someplace' with me?"

Thomas nodded eagerly.

"Climb in, then. I have news for you."

Dolly clippity-clopped to the Duke of Gloucester Street, where Nicholas left horse and wagon and led Thomas into Wetherburn's Tavern and asked for hot cider for both of them. Thomas shivered until the fire in the fireplace warmed him through and he had both hands wrapped around a steaming tankard. Only then did Nicholas start his tale.

"I was looking in on David Greenwall, out on Jamestown Road, today," he said. "You know him?"

"He has bad lungs," Thomas said.

Nicholas smiled faintly. "You have a good head for patients, Thomas. I predict you'll be a doctor someday. But that isn't the point of my story, is it?"

For a quiet man, Nicholas could certainly take a long time to tell a thing, Thomas had always thought. He squirmed in his fiddleback chair.

"I have been asking all of my patients if they have seen

anyone matching Patsy's description. All of them have said no—except David Greenwall."

Thomas set down his tankard.

"He and his wife were on their way back from Hampton some days back," Nicholas went on, "and they spotted a little girl on the side of the road—all alone. They stopped and asked her where she was going and if she needed a ride, but she wouldn't talk." Nicholas leaned forward. "Now that sounds like our girl, doesn't it?"

"What happened?" Thomas asked. He was drumming his fingers impatiently on the cherrywood table.

"She pointed in the direction of Williamsburg, so they took her into their wagon, thinking she would continue to point the way."

"Did she?"

"No. When they reached the outskirts of town, she jumped out and ran away."

"They should have followed her!" Thomas said fiercely.

"At least we know what direction she hails from, eh? We can thank God for that."

Thomas felt a flutter. He hadn't been consulting God much. He scraped his chair back from the table and jiggled his knees. "I have to go and tell Caroline."

Nicholas agreed, and they left their half-full tankards on the table and headed with Dolly to the Taylors' house on North England Street.

The cozy home with its polished furniture and pleasantly creaky floors was one of Thomas's favorite places to be. But as he and Nicholas stood on the front steps, ready to knock, an unfriendly sound came from behind the wood blinds on the window of Robert Taylor's study to the left of the front door.

"The British are going to win the war!" Mr. Taylor shouted in that same angry stranger's voice Thomas had heard him use the night they'd found Patsy. "They don't need your help!"

"You don't know the passion of the Patriots, Father!" Alexander yelled back. "America has produced strong-minded people. They won't give up the fight easily!"

"Reason has given way to bloodshed and treachery!" came Robert Taylor's angry reply. "And I won't have you being a part of it! The British will win, and fairly. They do not need you spying on the Americans for them!"

Thomas was by now clutching the doorknob so hard that his knuckles had turned white. Gently, Nicholas peeled his fingers away and said close to his ear, "I think this is a private conversation. We'd best move on."

Thomas's body may have left the Taylors' front steps, but his thoughts didn't. As Nicholas drove him home in the wagon, the argument between Alexander and his father pounded over and over in Thomas's head. And so did the questions.

Is it true, what Mr. Taylor was saying? Does Alexander want to be a spy—for the British?

Is he lying to Sam—or to his father?

Only one thing was clear to Thomas: His father wouldn't be so confused. He would already have figured out a way to juggle all these burdens.

I've failed, Thomas thought miserably. His chest ached for his father.

When they reached the Hutchinsons' house, Thomas was wrestling so hard with his thoughts that he almost missed seeing Malcolm dart in front of them on his way somewhere. Malcolm suddenly stopped and saluted smartly in front of the wagon.

"Just reporting in, *sir,*" he said. "I'm on my way to see Mistress Patsy, as you *ordered.*"

Then he took off along the Palace Green and was gone.

Nicholas cocked his head curiously and watched him go. "He's been acting strange of late." He glanced sideways at Thomas. "But then, perhaps all of us have. This war has got us all carrying more than our share of the load, eh?"

Thomas looked at him sharply. Had Nicholas been reading his mind?

But before he could answer, the clop of hoofbeats and the squeak of a carriage drew their attention up the street. Making its way around the corner toward the Palace Green was the Hutchinsons' coach-and-four from the plantation. Thomas felt a rush of something pleasant—like warmth and hope and safety all wrapped into one.

It was Papa, coming home.

✝ ✦ ✝

Chapter Fourteen

Papa reined in the horses and called, "Well, here's a piece of good fortune!" He nodded and smiled broadly at Thomas and Nicholas. "My son and the good doctor here to meet us! You'll stay for supper, then?"

Nicholas smiled shyly and clucked Dolly to the side of the road.

"Us?" Thomas said.

Papa nodded toward the inside of the carriage. "I've brought your brother Clayton home with me. You might give him a hand getting out. He wasn't feeling well when we left the plantation."

For a guilty moment, Thomas's heart sank an inch or two. Supper with Mama, Papa, and Nicholas after such a confusing day sounded peaceful and comforting. Adding Clayton meant adding a sermon every other minute, along with plenty of disapproving looks and tongue clicks in between.

I need to talk to Papa alone, he thought as he jumped down from Nicholas's wagon and went for the carriage door. *I need his help, and I can't ask him with Clayton around, shaking his finger.*

But it wasn't only Clayton's finger that was shaking when Thomas opened the coach door. His pale, gray-eyed brother seemed to be trembling all over, and Thomas could hear his breathing from across the carriage. It was louder than his voice, as he whispered, "Good evening, Thomas."

Thomas rocked the carriage as he climbed up to the step. "You're sick!" he said. "I'll get Dr. Quincy to look at you!"

"No. Just help me out," Clayton said. "Just help me into the house, and I'll be fine."

Thomas put out his hand, and Clayton grasped it. As he helped his brother out of the carriage, Thomas could feel his bones even through his velvet waistcoat. Clayton had always been thin and frail, but now he reminded Thomas of the skeleton in Francis's shop. He chewed the inside of his mouth as he guided Clayton to the ground.

Inside the house, Mama had candles lit in the parlor, and her face glowed more golden than their flames as she bustled back and forth between squeezing Papa's hands and supervising Esther's placement of the trays on the table that had been pulled to the center of the room.

"We thought this couch by the window would be more comfortable for the travelers than the dining room," she said as Thomas brought Clayton into the cheerful room.

"Your father says you haven't been feeling well—"

She gasped, and Esther let out a cry. Thomas saw what they saw, and he felt his heart stop.

In the light of the candles and the fire in the corner fireplace, Clayton's face was the color of ashes, and his gray eyes were sunk deep in their sockets. Dr. Quincy was at his side at once with Mama right behind him.

"Clayton!" she cried. "Nicholas, he looks wretched!"

"I had no idea!" Papa said. "Clayton, why didn't you stop me on the road?"

Dr. Quincy was already digging into his bag as Mama and Papa half-carried Clayton to the couch. The doctor nodded to Thomas, and Thomas went to work.

While Mama watched, clinging to Papa and dabbing at her eyes with the corner of her dress, Thomas propped Clayton up and loosened his clothes. Nicholas listened solemnly to his heart and handed Esther a packet to be heated in a broth. Thomas didn't have time to wonder if she could manage to do it without burning it. He was busy opening the windows to let in air and slapping Clayton's hands, as Nicholas instructed, to keep the blood moving. He took turns with the doctor spooning heartsease syrup into his brother's mouth.

Before long, the gray disappeared from Clayton's face, and his lips stopped trembling. Nicholas murmured, "Thank you, Lord," as Clayton began to breathe normally again. The tea arrived, and everyone else's breathing came more easily, too.

"What happened?" Mama asked. "Are you all right, son?"

As she smothered Clayton's face with kisses, the doctor turned to Papa.

"That was a bad spell, wasn't it?" John Hutchinson said.

Nicholas nodded gravely. "His heart is too weak for the kind of work he's doing. But I know it's necessary in these times. We all have our burdens to bear."

"He shouldn't have to bear a burden so heavy it costs him his life!" Papa said.

"As long as we have enough dried calendula and heartsease syrup, it won't," Nicholas said.

Papa nodded and absently put his hand on Thomas's shoulder. "I saw that with my own eyes. That was a miracle you two just performed."

"We three," Nicholas said. "God was surely with us."

By then lids had been pulled off serving dishes, and porringers and chargers were piled with venison stew, batter bread, and spiced apples. Thomas took a double helping of those, because he knew they'd come from Caroline's kitchen. But as he balanced his plate on his lap, he thought about what Nicholas had just said—about everyone having burdens to bear.

Clayton certainly has one, Thomas thought. *And Papa has more than his share. I have plenty, too, but I can handle mine just as well. I can't load them on Papa like I had thought.* He took another mouthful of deer meat and chewed with decision. *I can bear burdens—Alexander's and Sam's and Caroline's and Lydia's and Francis's. And I can do it by myself.*

He turned his attention to the chatter going on around

him. Mama was enchanting Clayton and Nicholas with a tale about taking bandages she and Esther had made down to the hospital and meeting a gracious young officer who was thrilled with their contribution. Thomas stifled a snort.

Papa sat in a red wing chair by the fireplace, going through the messages that had come in while he was away. One of them brought a fierce frown to his face.

"What is it, John?" Mama said. "Not bad news, I hope."

"It is as far as I'm concerned," he said gruffly. He strolled restlessly to the window and looked out into the gathering darkness. "It seems that Samuel is not doing well at school."

"Samuel?" Clayton said. "Why, he was always such an excellent student."

"*Was* is the correct word," Papa said. "According to the headmaster, Samuel is now more interested in staring out the window during class and carrying on lively discussions during study hours than he is in getting a proper education."

"I sent him some baked goods," Mama said hopefully. She blushed and looked at her lap as if she'd been silly.

Everyone sat in an uncomfortable silence, Thomas the most uneasy of all. He concentrated on his batter bread and tried not to meet anyone's eyes. *I have to bear Sam's burden,* he told himself. *I promised him.*

"Perhaps you would be interested in the quest we are on," Nicholas said.

Everybody looked at him gratefully.

"Who are 'we,' sir?" Mama said.

"Thomas and Caroline and Malcolm. And myself."

"And what is the purpose of this quest?" Papa said.

Thomas could tell by his thin smile that he was pulling his attention away from Sam's bad school marks only to be polite. But by the time Nicholas had finished telling the story of Patsy and their search for her family, every eye was on him—especially Clayton's.

"The way you've described this little waif," he said, "sounds exactly like a girl I saw in Yorktown last summer, when I fetched Malcolm from the ship the *Mary Jones.*" He looked a little sheepish. "I suppose that sounds rather mad."

"There must be hundreds of little black-haired girls in Virginia with sad eyes, Clayton," Papa said. "This is a sad time."

Clayton shook his head. "I know, but not like this one, Father. Her eyes were the green of sea water, and they held me. I wanted to do something for her. She seemed so alone coming off that big ship."

"How lovely, Clayton," Mama said.

And how odd! Thomas thought. It wasn't like Clayton to want to take in lost children—not unless they minded their manners. But if it really had been Patsy, who could blame him? Thomas himself had carried her on his back, after vowing he would never even *touch* a girl.

"You should ask Malcolm," Clayton said. "He could barely take his eyes off her long enough to introduce himself to me."

Thomas drooped. "It couldn't have been Patsy, then," he said. "Malcolm had never seen her before the day she was shot."

"Indeed, if they were on the same ship all the way from Scotland, he would have recognized her," Papa said.

Clayton shrugged and nodded toward the pile of messages John Hutchinson had left on the table. "What other news do you have, Father?"

Papa grunted. "None I can trust. The rest are from Xavier Wormeley."

Thomas began to study his spoon. *I can't look at him,* he told himself. *I can't tell him what Xavier has done to Francis. I promised.*

"I suppose it's good for a laugh, though, eh?" Papa said. He uncurled a piece of paper, a page torn from a ledger to save scarce paper, and laughed harshly. "He reports that there is a Loyalist spy here in Williamsburg, a Loyalist claiming to be a Patriot and then passing Patriot secrets to the British."

"That's ridiculous!" Clayton said. "Surely if there were such a person you would know about him. You are in such close touch with the Loyalists."

Thomas kept his eyes riveted on the spoon. He was certain everything he knew about Alexander was scrawled across his face as clearly as if it were in his copybook.

"I've been gone from town a great deal," Papa said. "It is possible that some such thing has happened in my absence, though it's much more likely that this is some figment of Xavier Wormeley's twisted imagination. He will never rest until he has driven the last of them from town —or had them hanged!"

"Idle talk then, you think?" Clayton said.

"I hope it's no more than that," said John Hutchinson. "I hope Xavier is not planning to take any action on this without proof. He has blundered more than once and almost ruined people's lives. Thomas?"

Thomas nearly leapt from his chair. His father's eyes drilled into him.

"You are in more parts of this town than anyone else I can think of," Papa said, "making your deliveries for Francis. Suppose you keep your ears open, eh, and tell me of anything you may hear about these so-called Loyalist spies? I would like to stay one step ahead of Xavier Wormeley."

Thomas knew he was staring stupidly at his father, but he couldn't answer. He wasn't sure which one of his promises he would be breaking if he agreed.

"Well, son?" Papa said, his heavy brows drawing together over his deep-set blue eyes.

But before Thomas could untangle his tongue, Clayton gave a cry from the couch. He was looking out the window, and he frantically waved a bony hand.

"There she is!" he said.

"Who, Clayton?" Mama hurried to the window and pulled back the curtain.

Thomas nearly cried out himself. There, crossing the yard, was Malcolm. On his back, he carried a laughing Patsy.

"That's the girl I saw coming off the ship!" Clayton said. "She's right there in the yard!"

✢ ✢ ✢

Chapter Fifteen

Thomas was frozen to his chair. Everyone else, however, burst into action.

Mama bustled to the couch to calm Clayton, and Papa strode out the front door to beckon Malcolm and Patsy inside. Nicholas studied the scene from the window, while Esther stood in the middle of the parlor saying, "Malcolm wouldn't lie! Malcolm wouldn't lie!"

Malcolm followed Papa into the parlor. Patsy's hands were clenched so firmly around his neck that Thomas wondered how Malcolm could breathe.

If he's anything like me right now, Thomas thought, *he can't breathe anyway.* He felt sorry for Malcolm, with all those adult eyes on him, demanding answers. His old feelings of friendship for Malcolm swept over him.

"Why don't you set Patsy down here on the chair?" Nicholas said gently.

"Yes, sir," Malcolm said, and he started for the wing chair by the fireplace, but Patsy started to whimper.

"Oh, you precious child, you're frightened!" Mama said. "It's all right, little lamb. No one is going to hurt you."

Patsy, however, didn't appear to believe her. As soon as Malcolm let go of her, she sent up a wail. Her arms flew out to Malcolm, and then, to Thomas's dismay, to him.

"Go to her, Thomas," Mama said. "She's afraid."

Reluctantly, Thomas went to the chair, and at once Patsy wrapped her arms around his leg and wouldn't let go. He stiffly patted her head, and she quieted down.

"Malcolm, had you ever seen Patsy before the day you discovered her in Peggy Cheswell's stable?" Papa asked. His pointed gaze didn't leave Malcolm's face.

Malcolm looked right back at him without so much as a twitch of an eyelash. "Why would you ask me that, sir?"

"Because," Clayton cut in, "we both saw her the day I came to fetch you from the *Mary Jones*. You came down the gangplank with her!"

"Excuse me, sir, but I believe you are mistaken," Malcolm said.

"You're certain?" Papa said.

"That was the girl," Clayton cried. "I know it!"

Suddenly, Esther marched across the room and stood by Malcolm. "I know the lad, Mr. Hutchinson, sir," she said. "He's a good boy, and I've never known him to lie."

"You've known him all of four months!" Clayton said.

Esther turned her head and fastened a cold gaze on the oldest Hutchinson son. Thomas had a feeling she was seeing him in his baby dress, crawling across the floor.

"Excuse me, Master Clayton," she said icily, "but I pride myself on my judgment. Otis and I think of Malcolm as our own son. I pray you not to question him—or us."

Thomas didn't think he'd ever really loved Esther before, but at that moment, he wanted to run up and . . . well, perhaps not hug her . . . maybe offer to scrub her pots. . . .

Clayton felt no such rush of love, it was obvious. He pulled himself up like an indignant rooster, and it took both of Nicholas's hands to pull him back.

"Father!" Clayton cried.

"Thank you, Esther," Papa said.

"I can tell you, Mr. Hutchinson—"

"*Thank* you, Esther," he said firmly.

Even Esther, who had nursed every male Hutchinson in the room, knew when to be quiet. She sniffed and folded her arms across her ample chest. Papa turned to Malcolm.

"I am sure there is a good reason for the difference between my son's memory and yours. Whatever that is, I see no choice but to let this matter rest. Trying to beat some other answer out of you to satisfy Clayton would do no good that I can see."

Thomas decided he really would hug Esther—sometime.

"I'm sorry, Nicholas," Papa said, "but it looks as if your search must continue."

"We're no worse off than we were before," the doctor said.

Mama glanced nervously out of the window over Clayton's angry head. "It's dark, Malcolm. You should be getting Patsy back to Peggy Cheswell's. Esther, would you wrap up some spiced apples for them to take along?"

Esther didn't look happy about leaving Malcolm's side, but she left in a huff, and Malcolm nearly ran to Patsy to peel her arms from around Thomas's leg. Thomas wanted to say something to him, maybe "I'm glad they didn't try to bully you" or perhaps "Can't we be friends again?" But Malcolm wouldn't meet his eyes. He packed Patsy on his back and left.

When he was gone, Clayton slapped his hand against the sofa cushion. "I must say, I feel as if *I've* been called a liar."

"Clayton, please don't upset yourself," Mama said.

Nicholas nodded. "Your mother is right. That medicine will do no good if you're going to go into a frenzy, eh?"

"What would you do in my place?" Clayton cried. His voice was winding up to a feverish pitch. "I know what I saw!"

"Why would Malcolm lie and say he never saw her if he did?" Papa asked. "It is apparent to me that he cares quite deeply for the girl. Why wouldn't he reveal everything he knew in order to find her family?" He fixed his eyes on Clayton. "Let us put the matter to rest."

Long after everyone else had turned in and even Papa's candle in his study had been blown out, Thomas lay awake in the autumn chill of his room and thought of nothing but Malcolm and Patsy.

Everyone loves Patsy, he thought as he squirmed to get warm under his pile of quilts. *Mama was ready to adopt her. Caroline will cry when we do find her family—I know she will—because that will mean she has to go away.*

He squeezed his eyes shut so as not to think of himself carting Patsy around on his back up and down the streets of Williamsburg, but the picture was there, and it wasn't such an embarrassing one, really.

I like her, too, he admitted to himself. But Malcolm liked her more than anyone, and he had from the first moment he saw her. Thomas remembered how angry Malcolm had been at Peggy Cheswell when he found out she'd shot Patsy. And hadn't he been the one to suggest giving her a name? Who was the first person he'd tried to protect when Walter Clark was shooting his gun in the woods?

A new thought came into Thomas's mind. *Malcolm never had a real family, not like Caroline and I do. His mother died when he was a little boy, and his father was a thief who taught him how to steal, too. That must be why he's taken to Patsy so, because he knows how it feels to be alone. He needs a family.*

Before he knew what was happening, Thomas was crying. Hot tears were burning their way down his cheeks. All Thomas could think was, *He must hate me for trying to boss him around. I don't want him to hate me.*

There was only one way to stop the tears. Thomas whipped off the covers and scrambled out of bed. He pulled on his breeches and carried his shoes down the stairs with him. He slipped them on at the back door and crept across the yard toward the kitchen building where Malcolm slept on a pallet on the floor in front of the fireplace.

The kitchen was dark, as Thomas had expected, but when he put his hand on the doorknob, he was startled to hear a voice inside. It was whispering, but Thomas knew it was Malcolm's. Who was he talking to at this hour?

Thomas considered peering in the window, but Malcolm's sharp eyes would surely see him. Instead, he slid down behind a water barrel that stood in front of the kitchen and strained his ears to listen.

"Don't be afraid," Malcolm was saying. "They almost believed Clayton at first, but I changed their minds. There's no need to run away again. Where would you go anyway?"

There was a low mumbling from someone else. Thomas huddled in closer.

"I think I've convinced everyone that you're an orphan and have no family after all," Malcolm said. "Caroline seems ready to give up the search. Only Thomas is bein' stubborn."

The other voice mumbled.

"These are good people here in Williamsburg," Malcolm said. "I know one of them will take you in, and we will at least be in the same town. What about Peggy Cheswell? Perhaps she'll just keep you—"

At the very same instant that Thomas realized who Malcolm was talking to, a girlish voice chirped from inside the kitchen in a Scottish lilt. "I don't want to live with Peggy Cheswell forever and ever! I don't like her! She only lets me stay there because she feels guilty for shootin' me!"

Patsy! Patsy was talking? Thomas held his head as the thoughts stormed in. *That's why Malcom called her that— it's her name. That's why he has given up looking for her family. He wants her to stay here in Williamsburg.*

The next thought went through him like a woodchopper's ax: *Malcolm lied. He lied to us all.*

The rush of warm, friendly feelings . . . the hot tears of longing to talk to Malcolm again . . . the pride in the Scottish boy for standing up bravely to Clayton and the rest— all of that left him, and left him empty and angry.

It had been a long time since his old anger had crept up his backbone and bristled at his neck, but it happened now, so fast that he was standing up, ready to burst into the kitchen before he knew what he was going to do.

But he had barely begun to hurry out from behind the water barrel when he heard footsteps, sounding as angry as he felt, stomping across the yard.

"Someone's coming!" Malcolm hissed from inside the kitchen. "Out the window, Patsy!"

There was less rustling about than Thomas would have expected from two people climbing out a window, one of them with a bandaged foot. Then the kitchen was quiet. Thomas wanted to run after them, catch them at their secret game, but he barely had time to duck behind the water barrel again before the feet marched up the steps. The door was thrown open, and Esther cried, "Malcolm Donaldson, I want to talk to you!"

But no one answered. "Humph!" she said, and marched back toward the house.

Thomas squirmed out of his hiding place and ran to the back of the kitchen. But the yard was quiet.

✢ ⋅✢⋅ ✢

Chapter Sixteen

Thomas tossed and turned in his feather bed that night until tufts of goose down floated in the air, but the answer to the question—*What do I do now?*—wouldn't come to him. He finally got up and padded across the cold plank floor to the window and looked out over a sleepy Williamsburg.

I wonder if Papa ever walks the floor at night, worrying about his problems, he thought.

He imagined his father in his library, sitting at his desk with a candle burning. His head was bent and his hands were folded. He was praying—of course.

Thomas bent his own head and folded his own hands, but it had been such a long time, and God seemed very far away. He couldn't seem to say the words or think the prayer thoughts. The only thing that came into his head was the thought of Caroline, her brown eyes filled with ideas. It made the burden suddenly seem lighter.

Malcolm thinks he's so smart, Thomas thought as he charged to the Taylors' house early the next morning, an angry puff of frosty air exploding from his lips with every breath. *He doesn't need me keeping secrets for him.*

Besides, he was tired of carrying so many things alone. He needed someone now. He needed Caroline.

He was prepared to throw pebbles at her bedroom window until she poked her head out, but as he rounded the corner, he was delighted to see her already outside, about to climb her favorite tree.

"Caroline!" he called to her.

It wasn't until she turned around that he saw that her face was blotched and puffy, with the marks of fresh tears on her cheeks. Thomas felt his stomach clench. There had been a time when Caroline never cried. Now it seemed there were tears every day.

"What's the matter?" he said when he got to her.

She sank to the ground with her skirt mushrooming around her and gathered her red cape miserably about her shoulders. Thomas kicked at a stone and watched her. He felt as if there were something squeezing his insides.

"Everything," she said tearfully.

"Is it your father?" Thomas asked. "Did he yell at you again, the way he did that night—?"

"Not at me!" Caroline cried. "At Alexander!" She looked up at him out of a streaming face. "Oh, Tom, they had the most awful fight!"

Thomas sat stiffly a little apart from her. "What did they fight about?"

"Alexander told Papa that he wanted to join the British and help them."

"You mean, join Cornwallis's army in Carolina?"

She shook her head. "No. He said if he did that, Xavier Wormeley would run Mama and Papa and me out of town, or do something worse to us. Alexander said he wanted to pretend to be a Patriot so he could get secrets from them and tell them to the British—"

Suddenly, Caroline covered her melon-slice mouth with her hand, and her eyes grew round as wafers. "I shouldn't have told you that!" she cried. "But I've kept it a secret for so long! Papa and Alexander fight every night. It's made Papa so angry all the time." She turned her swollen eyes to Thomas. "Oh, Tom, please don't tell anyone! I don't want Alexander to be hanged!"

"Hanged?"

"I read about it in the newspaper. When people are caught spying against the Patriots, they *hang* them!"

Thomas shook his head. "I won't tell. I promise."

Caroline's tears stopped. "Papa said he forbid Alexander to do such a thing. He said the British are going to win anyway, and everything will go back to the way it was before, and for Alexander to let it be a fair and honest fight." Her eyes widened again. "Do you know what naive means, Tom?"

Thomas felt his chest puff out a little. "It means you think like a child, because you don't know all the facts. Alexander taught me that," he added.

"Well, Alexander told Papa he was naive. He said if the Patriots win, everything is going to change, so we have to do all we can to stop it." She looked down at her tiny hands, folded in her lap. "Do you hate me now because my brother is talking against your side?"

Thomas was stunned. *Hate* Caroline? He looked at her, with her eyes all ringed with red from tears, her nose like a cherry from the morning cold, her mouth quivering as if she was going to cry again. *How could I ever hate Caroline? She's my best friend.*

"Do you, Tom?" she said.

"Don't be a ninny, Caroline," he said, and shrugged. "So what happened after that?"

"Alexander slammed out of the house—and he's still gone! I was waiting out here for him to come back."

Thomas chewed on his lip. *Alexander has run off to be a spy. But for the Loyalists, like he told his father? Or for the Patriots, like he told Sam?*

Caroline was watching him. "What, Tom?"

Thomas's mind spun like Mr. Taylor's windmill. "He probably went someplace to think," he said. "He'll be back."

"Do you really think that?"

"Yes," he said, and he got to his feet. "In fact, I'd better go, because Alexander will be along for lessons soon and I have to be ready. I haven't even read the newspaper yet like he told me to."

She studied Thomas with her round, brown eyes as he backed away. "Will you tell me if you see him?" she said.

"Sure."

"Do you promise?"

He didn't answer as he ran up North England Street toward home. The burden was strapped firmly on his back again.

But he didn't go home. When he was out of her sight, he tore across the Palace Green and past the church to the college. It was barely seven o'clock, and a stream of sleepy-eyed students in their black robes began trickling into the classrooms. Thomas bypassed them all and took the steps three at a time to Sam's floor. He tapped on his door and looked around while he waited. Maybe Alexander was at this very minute hiding in some doorway, waiting for Sam to come out.

And then his heart seemed to slam to a halt. There was no answer at the door.

Thomas knocked again, louder this time, and then pushed open the door. The first thing he saw was Sam's black student's robe hanging over the back of the chair.

Thomas flew across the room and tore into the unmade bed. But he knew there would be nothing under the pillow when he stuck his hand there. The bundle was gone.

Thomas stood frozen, and for a moment all he could think was, *He won't have any soap when he gets where he's going. How will he stay clean?*

He sank to the floor with the pillow still in his hands and pushed his face into it.

What should I do? I have to tell Papa. No, I promised Sam. But if I tell Papa, maybe he can find Sam and bring him back before he goes very far. And Alexander, too.

Thomas brought his face up and stared blindly. Another thought struck him. *What if Alexander really is a British spy? What if he's leading Sam straight into danger?*

He didn't want to believe that, and he shook his head until it hurt. But the thought wouldn't go away.

"Whose burden do I bear now?" he said out loud. *If it's Sam's, he could get hurt or even killed! And if it's Caroline's —if I don't tell what she heard Alexander say—Sam could get hurt or even killed!*

Throwing the pillow, Thomas scrambled to his feet and rushed from the room, the building, the college. By the time he reached his front door, gasping for air, his mind was made up. It was time to share the burden with Papa.

When he skidded to a stop in the front hallway, the only person there was Malcolm, about to go upstairs with an armload of firewood. The memory of last night—of Patsy and Malcolm in the kitchen—flashed through his mind, but he pushed it aside.

"Do you know where my father is?" he asked.

"Yes," Malcolm said coldly and continued up the steps.

"Where?" Thomas cried.

"He's on his way to Yorktown, to the plantation."

"No!"

Malcolm stopped and looked over his shoulder. "Yes. He left an hour ago."

The world careened to a stop, and Thomas sat heavily on the bottom step. He could hear Malcolm shifting the heavy load of wood in his arms.

"He had to go," Malcolm said, with a little more warmth

in his voice. "Nicholas says Clayton is too weak to be travelin' and goin' back to his work. Your papa had to go and see to things." He paused. "I'm sure he still means for you to be in charge, sir."

"Stop it!" Thomas cried. "I don't care about that!"

He shot from the steps and dove across the hall into the dining room. There was no sign of Alexander or his satchel or his books. Tears blinding his eyes, he stumbled back into the hall. Malcolm was on the first landing.

"Is Nicholas still here?" Thomas said.

"No, he said he was going to see Patsy. Thomas—"

But Thomas didn't wait. He was running up the Duke of Gloucester Street before Malcolm could get the rest of the sentence out.

I have to find Nicholas! he told himself as he ran. *I can't trust Malcolm, not after he lied about Patsy.*

He took the corner at Francis Street and wiped the last of the tears from his face. *Papa is gone. Clayton is too sick. I have to find Nicholas.*

He was passing the Clarks' house with Peggy Cheswell's in sight when the door to the ramshackle home flew open and Lydia Clark came to the top of the steps.

"Boy?" she called out to him in a voice that barely carried across the yard. "Could I have a word with you?"

Thomas glanced anxiously toward the Widow Cheswell's. There was no sign of Nicholas leaving. "I'm in a hurry, ma'am," he said to Lydia.

She groped nervously at her bedraggled curls. "Oh, please, this won't take long. I need your help."

Who doesn't? Thomas wanted to say. But he stopped and shifted from one foot to the other. She crept closer, looking over both shoulders as she came.

"What's your name?" she asked.

"Thomas," he said. "Thomas Hutchinson. But I really have to go—"

"You seem like a kind boy. The way you were with the little girl, and you asked about my husband—"

Thomas edged away. "Yes, ma'am, but—"

"Have you seen him?" she blurted out. "Have you seen my husband today?"

The break in her voice caught him, and he stopped edging. "Why?" Thomas said.

"I woke up this morning, and he was gone." She looked over her shoulders again and whispered, "The gun is gone, too."

If Thomas had thought his mind had spun in circles before, it was nothing compared to the confusion that swirled around in it now. He squeezed his eyes shut to stop it, and it lurched to a halt on one word: *gun.*

"I haven't seen him, ma'am," Thomas said. And he raced off in the direction of the gunsmith's shop.

✝ ✦ ✝

Chapter Seventeen

*S*am *gone. Alexander gone. And now Walter Clark, too.*

But that wasn't all Thomas was thinking as he leaped over puddles and dodged the splashing from wagon wheels on his way to the gunsmith's.

Walter took his gun with him. Alexander told Sam, "The gun is the problem"—that some people had to sell their horses for a musket. And Alexander had tried to buy a gun—maybe for Sam, maybe for himself. . . .

As he climbed George Fenton's steps, Thomas hoped that the gunsmith could tell him something. He had to know if Sam had a gun to protect himself, wherever he was going.

George Fenton was in his back room standing at his rifling machine, which looked like a huge corkscrew. He was gnawing at his lower lip with his big front teeth.

"One of my young rescuers!" he said when he saw Thomas.

"I suppose you want to see how I cut the grooves to make a bullet spin in a gun barrel."

Thomas tried not to think about a bullet spinning at Sam. "I'd like that, sir," he said, "but I've come to ask you a question."

Mr. Fenton shook his sleek beaver head. "I can't sell you a gun, son. People will do just about anything to get a gun these days, but to send a boy in—"

"I don't want a gun!" Thomas said.

But George kept cutting his grooves and talking as if Thomas hadn't spoken a word. "Just yesterday, Alexander Taylor came in again, intent on buying that pistol he wanted. He traded me for it—something much more valuable than that weapon, I'll tell you." He stopped working and looked quickly at Thomas. "Of course, I tried to talk him out of it, but he was determined. I hope his mother knows about it and doesn't come in here wanting it back. Had to be from her family, the initials being DH and all."

"DH?" Thomas said. "Did you say DH?"

George fumbled at his waist and pulled out a chain. On the end of it dangled the globe-shaped gold watch—with Thomas's grandfather's initials proudly engraved on it.

Thomas could feel the color draining from his face and his mouth gaping open.

"There it is—DH." George looked at him curiously. "Is there something wrong, boy?"

Thomas wanted to snatch the watch from him and scream, "That's mine! That belongs to my family, not Alexander Taylor's!" But as quickly as he thought that, another thought—a stronger and more certain one—knocked it out of the way. *Sam gave Alexander the watch to get a pistol. So Sam must have a gun. He can protect himself.*

Yet as he dragged himself from the gunsmith's shop with George Fenton watching, befuddled, from behind the rifling machine, that thought was not comforting. Anger was slowly creeping up the back of his neck.

Papa forbade Sam to go and fight, he thought bitterly as he marched along. *But he did it anyway. And he sold something that belonged to Papa, that Papa gave him, to get a pistol. . . . Hmmm, a pistol.*

Thomas stopped in front of the Capitol Building and chewed at his lip. Walter Clark had taken a Brown Bess. Malcolm had said that was the best for fighting in the infantry, shoulder to shoulder. It was the dragoons who used pistols.

He shook his head. It didn't matter. What mattered was that he'd kept Sam's and Alexander's secrets, and now they'd done terrible things to have their way. He wanted to take their burdens and throw them at somebody.

"You there! Hutchinson!"

Thomas whirled from his daze. Swaying toward him from across the street, jowls flapping and cape blowing out behind him, was Xavier Wormeley. Thomas doubled his fists. *One hateful word from you,* Thomas thought angrily, *and I'll punch your flabby belly good!*

"What are you about here?" the magistrate said when he reached him.

"Walking," Thomas said. He straightened his shoulders and puffed out his chest.

Xavier folded his arms in front of him, though they barely

reached across his bulging front. "I saw you leaving the gunsmith's shop. What was your business there?"

"None of yours," Thomas replied.

Xavier's poke-hole eyes sank deep into his pudgy face, which turned a brilliant crimson color. "I will thank you to show me some respect, young man!" he bellowed.

Thomas didn't answer.

"I demand to know what you were doing in the gunsmith's shop!"

"Asking questions," Thomas said. "George Fenton wanted to show me how he drills a gun barrel."

Thomas made a move to walk away. Xavier wrapped his sausage fingers around his arm.

"You Hutchinsons think you are mighty clever!" he shouted. The smell of salt pork was so foul that Thomas gagged. "But I'm ahead of all of you this time, and I'm about to prove your almighty father wrong once and for all!" His eyes, what Thomas could see of them, glinted meanly. "I know that Alexander Taylor has not been seen since last night when he stormed out of his father's house. It is only a matter of time before I prove that he has gone off to spy for the British." He yanked Thomas so close to him that their noses almost touched. "If you know anything about this, you little Loyalist sympathizer, woe be unto you! I've thrown you in jail before, and I'll do it again!"

Thomas's neck burned as he recalled the time, several months earlier, when Xavier had thrown he and his father in jail on a false accusation. He wrenched his arm from Xavier's grasp and ran, pounding his feet into the ground and pumping his fists as if they were this moment driving one after the other into Xavier Wormeley's stomach.

"I'm warning you, Hutchinson!" Xavier screamed after him. "I'm warning you!"

Thomas had no idea where he was running. He only knew he had to get away from the magistrate before he hurled himself into him and started hitting. When he could no longer hear the shouts from behind him, Thomas slowed his steps and found himself in Peggy Cheswell's backyard. He threw himself onto the ground and began to hammer his fists into the mud. The second time his fist came up, a hand grabbed it and pulled him to his feet.

"Leave me alone, Xavier!" he cried.

But it wasn't Xavier who held him by both wrists and searched his face. It was Walter Clark.

"Did he say 'Hutchinson'?" Walter asked.

Thomas tried to wriggle away. "What do you want, Walter?" He tried to tug his arms from Walter's fingers, but the skinny man's hands were surprisingly strong.

"Did he call you 'Hutchinson'?" Walter asked again.

"Yes, that's my name! Now let me go!"

But Walter held fast and studied Thomas's face as if he were looking for a family resemblance. Thomas stopped struggling and stared back.

Walter's bloodshot blue eyes weren't angry and mean as Xavier Wormeley's were. They reminded him of Martha the cat's eyes when she was after someone's leg. They didn't waver as they scanned Thomas's features. Thomas held still and waited.

"Where did they go?" Walter said finally.

"Who?"

But before Walter could answer, a voice from inside the house whined, "Patsy? Is that you? Where have you gone, girl?"

Walter's eyes suddenly grew wild, and like Martha herself, he whipped his disheveled head around and took off, dragging Thomas behind him.

"Leave me be!" Thomas cried.

But Walter gave him a shove, and Thomas skidded across a wooden floor on his chest and landed against a wall. A door slammed, and only a solitary square of light came in from a small window. Thomas caught his breath and smelled the dingy odor of dirty water and old soap.

"Why have you pushed me into Peggy Cheswell's laundry?"

He tried to get up, but Walter caught him by the neck from behind with his forearm and clapped his hand over Thomas's mouth. With anger shooting up his spine, Thomas chomped down hard with his teeth. Walter yelped and took away his hand, but he held on hard with his other arm.

"Be still!" he hissed into Thomas's ear. "Please, be still!" His voice, like his eyes, wasn't stern, but something about it was frightening.

Thomas stopped squirming and nodded. "I'll be still."

"Good. That's good," Walter said. He gave a little laugh, but he squeezed Thomas tighter. "I don't want to hurt you. I don't hurt people, you know."

You could have fooled me! Thomas thought. His neck was already aching from being pulled backward.

"They say I do, but I don't," Walter went on. "But people don't pay attention when I ask them questions."

Thomas tried to nod, but Walter tightened his grip.

"I'll answer any question you want," Thomas said.

"Good." Walter gave his nervous laugh again. "That's good because I have a question for you—Hutchinson."

"Thomas," he said. But that didn't seem to be what Walter wanted to know.

"Are you Samuel's brother?" he asked.

"Yes."

Walter's laugh was gleeful this time. "Then you know where he is! Where has he gone with Alexander Taylor?"

Thomas's heart sank. With Walter's arm pinching his throat like a vice, he would have told him anything he wanted to know. But this was one question he didn't have an answer to. It was the one secret no one had told him.

"I don't know," he said. "My brother didn't tell me."

Walter jerked his neck so sharply that Thomas's feet came off the floor. "Yes, you do! I know you do! You Hutchinsons tell each other everything! Now where is he?"

"I told you, I don't know—"

"Please tell me. Don't make me hurt you, please." Walter's voice was pleading.

"I would tell you if I knew," Thomas said. "Honest!"

"They went off without me," Walter said fitfully. "I was supposed to go with them. The Virginia Militia wouldn't take me last summer. But Alexander, he said he would find me a place. He was finding one for Samuel Hutchinson, and he could find one for me."

Thomas held his breath and thought hard. *Maybe if I hold very still, he'll loosen up enough for me to pull away.*

"I took a gun and everything," Walter went on. He laughed his high-strung laugh. "I don't feel bad about it either. That gunsmith should support the war. He should!"

He gave Thomas's neck another jerk, and Thomas nodded as hard as he could.

"I was ready," Walter said. "And I went last night to tell them. And Alexander was gone. And Samuel was gone. They left without me!"

Thomas thought the man sounded just as Thomas himself used to when he was about to pick up the nearest item and pitch it in a fit of temper. That gave him an idea.

"They're bullies is all, Walter," he said. "But they can't get away with this. I'll help you find them."

Walter tensed. "You will?"

"Of course. They've played dirty tricks on me before, too."

Thomas waited, and slowly Walter's arm grew slack.

"Let's go find them," Thomas whispered.

He felt Walter nod, and the arm fell away from Thomas's neck. With a surge, Thomas scrambled away from him and flew for the door.

But before he could get his hands on the doorknob, he felt something hard come across his back. Thomas's breath rushed out of him, and he tumbled to the floor again.

When he rolled over, he was looking straight up the barrel of a Brown Bess.

☩ ⚜ ☩

Chapter Eighteen

"**W**hy did you do that?" Walter cried. He shoved the gun barrel closer to Thomas's face.

"I, uh . . . we were going to go look for Sam and Alexander. Remember?"

Walter's blotchy, brick-colored face twisted as if he were about to cry. "You were going to leave me behind, too!"

"No!" Thomas said.

He tried to sit up, but Walter knocked him back with the end of the gun. Thomas stared at it as his heart beat its way up to his throat.

"Please don't shoot me," he said.

"Then you tell me where they went without me!" Walter cried.

Thomas closed his eyes. He felt as if he were being crushed by every burden he'd tried to bear since they had found Patsy on this very property. Now he knew how she must have felt that day—hunted down like a wild animal. Only it was Walter who was the animal, and that was the most frightening thing. He wasn't behaving like a person at all.

"They didn't tell me," Thomas said desperately.

"No! I heard that the Hutchinsons tell each other everything! Xavier Wormeley told me that. He told me to tell him anything I heard, but I wouldn't. Samuel Hutchinson is my friend." Walter clutched at the gun, and it waved crazily. "But not anymore! Not when I find him!"

Thomas watched the gun barrel with terrified eyes. *I wish the Hutchinsons did tell each other everything,* he thought as the panic thumped in his throat. *If we did, I would have told Papa. I wouldn't be carrying this burden by myself. I wouldn't be about to die.*

And he was going to die—he knew it. Any second, Walter was going to squeeze the trigger of the Brown Bess too hard, and it was going to fire . . . right into Thomas's face.

Thomas's fear turned icy cold, and he could feel his last ounce of courage seeping away. He could feel himself giving up.

And then something happened. He began to pray.

Please, God, I don't know what to do. The burden is too heavy for me.

He searched the ceiling as if he were looking for God's answer printed there. Movement at the tiny square window caught his eye.

Thomas glanced back at Walter. He was staring at the

stock of his gun and muttering to himself. Thomas risked another look at the window. It was Patsy, peeking in with green eyes showing as much fear as he knew his own did.

Once more, Thomas's eyes darted to Walter. He was still staring at the gun and muttering. When Thomas looked back at the window, Patsy was gone.

Please, God, he prayed. *Let her go and get someone. Let her find Malcolm.*

There was a chance now, he knew. But it was going to take time for her to get someone, especially running on her wounded foot. He would have to stall. He took a deep breath and fastened his eyes on Walter again.

"I talked to your wife this morning," he said. "She's a nice lady."

Walter shook his head. "She doesn't love me."

"Oh, but she does," Thomas said, trying to keep his voice even. "She's very worried about you. She asked me to tell her if I saw you."

Walter smiled an empty smile. "No. You won't get away from me that way." He readjusted the gun. "Tell me where they went—Samuel and Alexander."

Thomas swallowed. "Do you want to know a secret, Walter?"

Walter slanted his eyes at him. "What secret?"

"A secret I know about Alexander Taylor."

Walter thought a minute and then said, "What is it?"

"Alexander Taylor can't be trusted."

"That's not true!" Walter cried out, and for an instant, Thomas thought he was going to shoot him after all.

"But they say he's a Loyalist spy, Walter!" Thomas said. "Maybe he was only going to lead you into a trap!"

To Thomas's amazement, Walter threw his head back and laughed, a dry, nervous laugh that sounded more like a skittish chicken than a man.

"That's what he wanted everyone to think!" Walter said happily. "Alexander is smart, you know. He even made his own father believe that he was going to spy for those evil British. But he's not! He's every bit a Patriot!"

For a moment, Thomas forgot that he was trying to stall Walter and found himself listening to him. He wanted to believe that what the strange man was saying was true.

"Do you know that for sure?" Thomas asked.

"I saw him do it," Walter said smugly.

"Do what?"

"Meet an American soldier behind the Governor's Palace and hand him a whole pile of blankets and bandages. I listened."

Walter stopped, as if he were waiting for Thomas to be impressed.

"Go on," Thomas said.

"I heard him say, 'These are for our men. If you need any more of my services, please send for me. You'll see that I can be trusted.'" Walter's face clouded over. "And you're saying he can't be! That isn't true! It isn't!"

Suddenly, everything happened at once. Walter jabbed the gun barrel into Thomas's chest, and with one fling of his arm, Thomas knocked it aside and twisted himself out of the way. Behind him he heard shouting.

"Drop it, sir—"

"Drop it, I say!"

A shot blasted through the tiny building, and there was thudding and bumping, and then the sound of boots hitting the ground outside and fading away.

Thomas didn't move. There was no pain—only the furious slamming of his heart.

"Thomas!" cried a familiar voice above him.

Thomas jumped and threw up his arms.

His father caught him against his chest and held on. "Are you all right, son?" John Hutchinson breathed into his neck.

"I think so, sir," Thomas said. He was beginning to shake, and he held his teeth together to keep them from chattering.

Behind them, a set of footsteps stopped at the door.

"I couldn't catch him, John," Robert Taylor said. "But I'll go to Xavier Wormeley."

"No, that's too dangerous for you," Papa said. "Let us go to my house, and we'll send Malcolm for him. It will give the man time to get his wits about him, eh?"

"I don't think the man *has* any wits!" Robert said.

Thomas wasn't sure whether they were talking about Xavier or Walter. Right now he didn't care. He was alive, and Papa was here. It was going to be all right.

"Thank you, God," he said to the ceiling.

At the Hutchinsons' house, Mama, Esther, and Betsy Taylor were clinging together in the doorway like three terror-stricken kittens. Virginia Hutchinson broke away from them and flew to Thomas the moment he and Papa and Robert Taylor came into sight.

"Are you all right?" she cried. She took his face in her hands and searched it and then started pressing his arms. "Are you hurt? Did he hurt you?"

Papa chuckled. "You should know, Virginia," he said. "In the last 10 seconds, you've felt every bone in the boy's body."

"I want Dr. Quincy to look him over, John," she said.

Thomas opened his mouth to protest, but Papa said, "If it will make you feel better, my dear. For now I think the poor boy needs some room to breathe, eh?"

Mama reluctantly let go of him, but as they approached the yard, Esther waddled down the walk and started in.

"My baby!" she cried, and engulfed Thomas in a hug until he thought he would smother. He was too surprised to pull away.

"Did you catch that wretched man?" asked Betsy Taylor ferociously. "Will he be locked away forever?"

Thomas did peek under Esther's arm to stare at her. Caroline's mother was even more soft-spoken than his own mama, but her pale fists were scrunched up and ready for a fight. If he hadn't still been shaking, he might have laughed.

"No, he got away," Papa said as they all crowded into the parlor and Esther forced Thomas to prop up on the couch. "But not for long. I saw one of Xavier's assistants on the way here and told him to get some men after Clark right away. I thought to send Malcolm, but now there is no need." Papa looked around. "Where is Malcolm?"

"He's upstairs with Caroline," Mama said. "They're helping Dr. Quincy with Clayton."

Thomas got to his feet. "I should go!"

"You'll do no such thing!" Esther cried. Then she bobbed her head at Papa and said, "Now, Master John, I shall respect your wishes, but I think—"

"And I agree, Esther," Papa said. "Thomas, you've carried enough for one day, eh? You rest now."

Something suddenly occurred to Thomas. "Sir, Malcolm told me you had gone on to the plantation."

"I had, but Malcolm soon caught up with me. Clayton had another bad spell, and Nicholas said I should be sent for."

"But no one told me!" Thomas said, trying once more to stand up.

"It happened right after you left," said Mama. "No one knew where you had gone, not even Malcolm."

"But what about Clayton?" he asked. "Is he—?"

"He's doing better," Mama said. "That Nicholas Quincy and his medicine, they do wonders."

"I want to help!" Thomas said. "That's my job!"

"Not right now, son," Papa said. He sat on the other end of the couch and looked down at his hands before he went on. Everyone else in the room seemed to be looking away, too.

"What is it?" Thomas said. His heart was starting to hammer in his throat again.

"Both your brother Samuel and Alexander Taylor have disappeared. No one has seen them since last night."

It was Thomas's turn to look down at his hands.

"I had just seen Clayton through his crisis, and Mr. Taylor and I had just put our heads together to discuss the matter of our missing sons," Papa continued, "when from my library window I saw Patsy burst into the yard and go running among the chickens shouting for Malcolm." He cocked an eyebrow at Thomas. "I was led to believe that the child couldn't speak, but we shall come back to that later."

"She looked hysterical," Robert Taylor said. "Your father and I rushed out into the yard, and she told us this fantastic tale about your being held at gunpoint in Peggy Cheswell's laundry."

"I had only to hear the name Walter Clark, and I knew she was telling the truth," said Papa. "That poor man has been bewildered ever since he brought his bride here in August. That is why the militia refused him. I thought he might someday hurt himself or someone else, but Xavier Wormeley insisted he was harmless."

Because he was trying to use him as one of his spies! Thomas thought. But as with Patsy's ability to talk, he would come back to that later.

"It seems we got there just in time," Robert said to his wife. "We broke open the door and found Walter Clark shoving his gun right into Thomas's chest."

There was a general gasp, and Thomas saw why. Robert produced the Brown Bess and lay it on the table.

"He didn't run away with it, then?" Thomas asked.

"We managed to wrestle it away from him just after it went off," said Papa.

Mama gave a cry. "Went off?"

"The only damage done was a hole in the Widow Cheswell's laundry wall," Robert Taylor assured her. "Thanks to little Patsy."

"How did she know Thomas was in there?" Betsy asked.

Everyone turned to Thomas. "She saw me through the window," he said. "I prayed she would go and tell someone . . . and she did."

"Desperate times call for desperate prayers," Papa said. "Thank the Lord this one was answered."

Mama cocked her pretty, dark head. "Where is our little heroine, anyway? I want to hug her neck!"

They all looked at each other blankly. All except Esther, Thomas noticed. She bit her lip and edged closer to the door, watching Papa all the while. Thomas, in turn, watched *her*—that is, until Papa turned and locked on to him with his sharp blue eyes.

"I know Walter Clark is a disturbed young man," Papa said, "but I suspect he did not pull you into that outbuilding and put a gun to your chest without some cause, however strange. Suppose you start from the beginning and tell me what led Walter to take you as his prisoner."

Thomas didn't take his eyes off his father, but his thoughts ran over each other in their attempts to get to him first. He put a stop to them all with one memory. It was the picture of him cowering in Peggy Cheswell's laundry room, looking up the barrel of a Brown Bess and wishing he had shared his burdens with Papa, no matter what Reverend Pendleton had said about the importance of carrying other people's burdens.

"Thomas, you must tell me," Papa said.

"I will, sir," he answered. He drew in a breath and began to talk.

He told him everything . . . about discovering Alexander in Sam's room . . . about Sam making him promise not to tell that Alexander had become a Patriot spy . . . and about Sam asking Thomas to bring information to him that might reassure him that Alexander could be trusted. He told of Walter stealing a gun and of his wife revealing that the militia didn't want him. It was hard, but he also told of how Sam had given Grandfather Daniel Hutchinson's watch to Alexander to buy him a pistol, and of how Walter, who claimed he was supposed to go with them, had assured Thomas that Alexander was, indeed, a Patriot now, because he had given supplies and pledged his service to an officer at the hospital.

Through it all, Thomas looked only at Papa. He knew what he would see if he looked at the Taylors. His words, he knew, were wounding them like musket shot. He was glad Caroline didn't appear in the parlor doorway until he was finished and the room was silent. Someone would tell her later—but he didn't want to be the one.

"I'm sorry, Robert," Papa said finally. "The only comfort I can offer is that now Xavier Wormeley has no reason to go after Alexander or to chase you and your family out of town."

Caroline ran to her mother, her face full of questions. Betsy hushed her with a finger to her lips.

"I appreciate that, John," Robert said. "Though I still find it hard to believe that Alexander would turn traitor." He looked around helplessly, and Thomas was sure he saw tears in his eyes. "I think we should be getting home,

Betsy," he said in a thick voice.

She nodded and took Caroline's hand. Thomas wanted to call to his friend as they moved toward the door, *Can we still be friends, Caroline? Please?*

And then Malcolm appeared, and another burden Thomas had been carrying suddenly felt like a lead weight on his shoulders. It didn't look as if he were the only one. Esther gave Malcolm a look as dark as a thundercloud and jerked her head to order him from the room.

But Papa said, "Malcolm, do you know where Patsy has gone?"

Malcolm looked stricken. "I, sir? Why would I know where she be, sir?"

Esther gave him a harsh poke, and John Hutchinson's eyebrows shot up. "You seem to have taken to the child. I thought perhaps—"

"No, sir," Malcolm said. "I don't know where she is. I came down to say that Master Clayton would like to see his parents."

Mama started for the door and turned to Betsy. "Please don't go," she said. "It's been such a trying day. Do stay and have dinner with us, and we'll talk of this some more."

"Yes, do," said Papa. "Perhaps we can think of a way to retrieve our wayward sons, eh?"

The Taylors all nodded listlessly as Mama and Papa hurried upstairs with Esther bustling after them. Malcolm started to follow, but Thomas took the parlor in three steps and stopped him in the hall. He could feel Caroline right behind him.

"*What* has happened?" she said, hands on hips. "Will someone please tell me?"

"Yes, Malcolm," Thomas said, "please tell us."

Malcolm turned from the bottom step and looked at Thomas. His eyes were full of hurt.

"Please?" Malcolm said. "Did you say *please*, Master Thomas?"

Thomas put his hands over his ears. "Stop it!" he cried. "I'm sorry I ordered you around! I was only doing what I thought I was supposed to do. I never meant to make you feel like a servant. You're my friend!"

"Am I?" Malcolm said.

"I thought you were—until I found out you lied to us."

Caroline tugged at Thomas's sleeve. "Lied? What are you talking about, Tom?"

Malcolm backed up a step.

"I heard you and Patsy in the kitchen last night," Thomas said. "You knew all along that she could talk . . . because you have known her ever since you were on the ship together!"

Caroline's eyes shot wide open. "Is that true, Malcolm?"

"No," said Malcolm. Thomas could see him swallow. "I've known Patsy much longer than that. She's my sister."

✣ ✢ ✣

Chapter Nineteen

𝔄t that moment, Thomas wasn't sure who he was or who was standing beside him. It was as if nothing was the same as it had been before Patsy—Patsy *Donaldson*—came along.

"Your sister?" Caroline said. "But Malcolm, why didn't you tell us?"

He looked straight at Thomas. "I tried to, the very next day, right here in this hall. But Thomas ordered me off to work. Later, I dragged him into the stable to tell him, but that went sour, too."

"I told you, I'm sorry," Thomas said.

Malcolm shrugged. "It's no matter anyway. It was my own burden to carry."

Thomas stared at him. "You have burdens, too?"

"Who among us does not, eh?" Malcolm narrowed his sharp black eyes at both of them. "You won't tell anyone, will you? If they find out, they'll make me tell where she's supposed to be and they'll send her back."

"No! They can't do that!"

Thomas looked at Caroline. She had flown right at Malcolm and was hanging on to the front of his shirt.

"We won't tell, Malcolm! I promise!" she cried. "They can't send her back there."

"Back where?" Thomas said, and then he shook his head. "You have to tell them, Malcolm. It's no good carrying this burden by yourself."

Malcolm shook his head. "You don't know, lad."

"Yes, I do! If I had told Papa all my secrets from the beginning, a lot of bad things wouldn't have happened. I wouldn't have had Walter Clark pointing a gun at me—"

Next to him, Caroline stamped her foot. "I don't care! You're safe now, Tom. Why does Malcolm have to tell and let them send Patsy back to those horrible people?"

Thomas looked down at the silver buckle on his shoe. "If I hadn't tried to carry all those burdens by myself, Sam and Alexander might still be here."

Caroline looked at him helplessly, her brown eyes swimming. She looked as mixed-up as he felt. But it was Malcolm who spoke.

"How do you know Patsy's master and mistress are horrible people, Caroline?"

There was a heavy step behind them, and Thomas turned to see Esther. She was looking straight at Malcolm, and her old eyes were stern.

"Have you told them yet?" she said to him.

Malcolm stuck his chin out and nodded.

Thomas felt his eyes bulging. "You told Esther, but you didn't tell us?"

"He only told me because Otis found him and his little sister cowerin' in the stables last night." She shook a gnarled finger at Malcolm. "I told you that you could trust Master Thomas, and his father, too. But you wouldn't listen to me. No, you had to carry it all by yourself."

"*Don't* listen to her, Malcolm!" Caroline cried. "What if they send her back there?"

Thomas put his hands over his ears and cried, "Stop! Everyone!" He fixed his eyes on Malcolm. "I did carry my burdens all by myself because I thought it was right, but it wasn't."

Esther looked at him and clucked her tongue.

Malcolm ran an anxious hand through his thick, black hair. "But the Reverend Pendleton said it—he said it in church—"

"'Bear ye one another's burdens,'" Thomas finished for him. To his surprise, Caroline repeated it with him.

"What about that?" Malcolm said. His voice broke like a fragile eggshell. "That comes from the Bible. I thought I was doin' right."

"I don't know," Thomas said. "I just know when it gets too heavy, you have to hand it over to somebody."

Malcolm shook his head. "I never done that in my life, lad."

"You never had anyone to hand it to before," said a voice from the top of the stairs. "But now you do."

As Papa slowly descended the rest of the steps with

Mama behind him, Malcolm darted his frightened eyes from Thomas to Caroline and back again.

"Tell him," Thomas whispered. "It will be all right. I promise." As Malcolm turned to look at Mr. Hutchinson, Thomas murmured something else. "God, please make this one promise I can keep."

When Papa reached them, he put a hand on Malcolm's shoulder.

"I have somethin' to tell you, sir," Malcolm said.

Papa ushered them all—including the Taylors—into the parlor, where they listened as Malcolm told his tale. Thomas felt a surge of pride at the way Malcolm the Mighty looked Papa straight in the eye as he confessed what he'd been hiding since the day Patsy was shot.

Ever since their mother had died when Patsy was a baby, it had been Malcolm's job to watch over the little girl. His father was always on the streets, stealing and bedeviling people, and Malcolm had tried to shelter her and teach her some of the things their mother would have wanted her to know.

But as he'd grown older and stronger, his father had insisted that he learn his trade—theft. When Malcolm had been arrested with his father, the court had ordered both Malcolm and his sister to be bound over as indentured servants to an American, rather than putting Malcolm in prison and Patsy in an orphanage. He could still remember the day, he said, when they found out that they had been split up between two families in Virginia. All the way across the ocean on the *Mary Jones,* Malcolm had assured her that it would be all right, that when they had both earned their freedom they would be together again.

But Patsy couldn't wait until she was 17. She had run away from the family she worked for and was looking for Malcolm in Williamsburg when she'd gotten lost. Peggy Cheswell had discovered her in her stable.

"I thought if everyone gave up the search and decided she was just a lost orphan with no family," Malcolm said, "someone would take her in and we would at least be near each other." For the first time, he looked away from Papa's piercing eyes. "I suppose now you have no choice but to send her back."

"No!"

All eyes turned to Caroline. She was standing up with her little fists doubled at her sides, her brown eyes blazing.

"Caroline!" Robert Taylor said.

But Caroline marched over to John Hutchinson and stood before him. "You can't send her back to that awful place, Mr. Hutchinson," she said.

Papa's demanding eyes grew a little softer. "We can't assume that Patsy's master and mistress are terrible task-masters, my dear," he said. "Mistress Hutchinson and I don't treat *our* servants harshly."

"But *they* do! I read it in the newspaper!"

The whole room looked mystified.

Papa cocked an eyebrow at her. "I don't understand, child."

Thomas saw Caroline's mobcap begin to quiver. "The first day I saw Patsy, I knew she was someone's servant by the dress she was wearing. So I read all the advertisements for runaway servants in the *Virginia Gazette,* and I found one I knew was describing Patsy. It said if anyone found her, they were to bring this criminal home—for her *just punishment!*"

"Why didn't you tell anyone?" Robert Taylor asked.

"I was going to tell Thomas, but I was angry with him because I knew he had a secret he wasn't telling me," she said. "And then Reverend Pendleton said we should bear one another's burdens. I thought that meant I should keep Patsy's secret."

She swept her eyes around the room at everyone, and Thomas was sure that if she'd had her basket with her, she'd have turned Martha loose on the lot of them. He caught Malcolm's eye, and the Scottish boy's lips twitched. He knew it, too.

Robert Taylor cleared his throat. "Perhaps there is something that can be done," he said.

Caroline squealed, and her father held up a warning hand. "I make no promises," he said. "But I will try. I may need your help, John, under the circumstances."

"Always," Papa said.

Caroline ran to her father, and he gathered her up on his lap. "I may have lost my son because I didn't listen to him," he said sadly. "I don't want to lose my daughter, too."

Dinner was somber, but somehow Thomas felt light, as if he'd been lugging firewood and someone had come along and taken it off his hands. And he could tell by the way Malcolm "accidentally" nudged him when he was pouring the bee balm tea that he was starting to forgive him. There would be a meeting of the Fearsome Trio again soon—he could feel it.

But it happened in a much different way than Thomas expected. After dinner, Robert and Betsy went home so Robert could get started on a letter to Patsy's master. Papa asked Caroline, Malcolm, and Thomas to join him in the parlor.

They looked nervously at each other as they seated themselves in front of him. To Thomas's surprise, Papa soothed them all with a rare smile.

"You're good children, all of you," he said. "And it pleases me that you've taken what Reverend Pendleton says so much to heart. Indeed, 'bear ye one another's burdens' does come from the Bible. Galatians, I believe."

"Chapter six, verse two," Malcolm put in.

Thomas and Caroline looked at each other. *He's still a show-off,* Caroline's eyes said.

Papa nodded his approval. "But did the good reverend also tell you about Jesus and His cross?"

They all shook their heads.

"When Jesus was taken to be crucified," he said, "He had a tremendous burden to bear. They forced Him to carry a cross twice His size through crowds of people who spit on Him and shouted insults. But Jesus never thought twice about whether it was right to carry that cross. He was obedient because He knew it was His Father's will."

He looked at each of them in turn with his penetrating blue eyes. "Did you ever question whether it was right for you to keep the secrets you were keeping?"

Thomas was the first to nod. He had wrestled with every promise until he was too tired to carry any of them.

"That is the difference between a cross and a burden,"

Papa said. "A burden is something that is thrust upon us by someone else. We struggle with it, and we question it, and we may even hate it because we're never sure that it's right. It's too heavy for us to carry alone." From the looks on their faces, he didn't have to ask if that was how they'd felt. "Carrying a cross brings us closer to other Christians. Shouldering a burden just brings on loneliness and fear— and that makes strangers of us all."

Thomas wanted to shout, "Yes!" It was always amazing how Papa could explain just exactly what he himself could never figure out.

"I want you to remember," his father said, "when something comes along that you think you should carry, ask yourself, *Is this a burden or a cross?* If it is a burden, it will cause nothing but pain . . . for everyone. If it is a cross, it will feel good and right."

"Mr. Hutchinson, sir?" Caroline said.

Thomas and Malcolm looked at each other. Of course she would have a question.

Her sandy eyebrows were knitted together. "How do we know the difference?"

"You go to God," said John Hutchinson. "He will let you know."

The air in the room was now clear for Thomas, and he drew in a long breath of it. He felt as if he could run up and down the Palace Green 10 times, and he would have, if Nicholas hadn't appeared in the parlor doorway. His pale blue eyes were heavy.

"John, I must talk to you," he said.

Papa stood up. "It's Clayton."

Nicholas nodded. "He's having another bad go of it."

"Can't you give him his medicine? That heartsease and the other?"

Calendula, Thomas filled in silently.

Nicholas rubbed the palms of his hands together as if what he were about to say was his burden. "I have none left," he said.

"We'll send Thomas to Francis—"

"I already sent Otis," he said. He shook his head. "Francis says he has none either."

"What?"

"I was as shocked as you are," Nicholas said. "But he wouldn't say why."

Thomas stared hard at the toes of his silver-buckled shoes. *I promised Francis I would never tell anyone, especially Papa. But is that a cross or a burden?*

Papa had started to pace the room, and he ran his thick hands through his hair in a way that was almost frantic.

"Sir?" Thomas said.

Papa glanced at him and then stopped. "You know something, son?"

Thomas nodded. "I do, sir."

And then he let go of the last of his burdens.

Papa took Thomas with him to the hospital at the Governor's Palace.

"You say you know where Francis's medicines are being kept?" Papa said to him as they hurried across the Palace Green.

"Yes, sir. In a glass-fronted cabinet in the ballroom."

John Hutchinson tightened his mouth into a grim line. "We will get heartsease and . . ."

"Calendula."

". . . if I have to break open the cabinet and steal it."

Thomas looked up at him. "Is that a cross, Papa?"

His father nodded. "That is a cross, Thomas."

The Palace showed none of the bustle of activity Thomas had seen there the day he'd delivered the last of the medicines. As Papa led him boldly inside, he saw that empty pallets were lined up along the walls, waiting for patients who had yet to come. Papa sniffed.

"Sure, they needed those medicines desperately, didn't they? People are dying here."

"There's the cabinet, sir," Thomas said, pointing.

Papa strode over to it and pulled open the glass door. He stood for a minute, looking puzzled.

"If these things are in such demand," he said to Thomas, "why is this cabinet not locked?" He shook his head. "We must find the person in charge and tell him what we need. Hopefully he will show some human kindness, eh?"

"If it's human kindness you want, you've come to the right place." A pair of shiny boots clicked across the ballroom floor and echoed amid its once-elegant walls. It was the officer to whom Thomas had delivered the medicines.

"May I help you, sir?" he said to Papa. His busy eyes passed over Thomas and then came quickly back. "You're the apothecary's apprentice! It's a pleasure to see you again."

He smiled. "Does Mr. Pickering want some of his donations back?"

Papa's eyebrows darted upward like a pair of arrows. "As a matter of fact, he does. My oldest son is very ill. If we don't have heartsease and calendula, he may die."

The smile disappeared. The officer gestured toward the cabinet. "Please, take anything you need! I wondered why the apothecary gave us so much when surely he has needs here in the town."

Papa stopped with his hand on the heartsease jar and looked at Thomas.

"He had to!" Thomas said. "There was an order from the army. I saw it!"

The officer frowned. "I know of no such order. I only know that the magistrate—" he put his hands out to show a fat man "—he sailed in here full of his own importance and said he knew an apothecary who would gladly give us anything we needed. He said he had great influence over the man, as he did on most of the townspeople."

Thomas could see his father's cheek muscles working to hold back his anger. There was no time for anger now. There was only time for Clayton.

"Get what we need, Thomas," Papa said. "I shall deal with Xavier Wormeley later."

☩ ⸱☩⸱ ☩

Chapter Twenty

"When will they be finished in there?" Thomas said impatiently. He got up from the steps and stared at the front of the courthouse.

"Looking at the door won't make it open," Malcolm said dryly.

"Know-it-all," Thomas said.

"Show-off," Malcolm answered.

"Stop it, you ninnies," Caroline said. But she smiled happily and smoothed her cape over her lap.

Thomas had to smile, too. It felt good to be the three of them again. No—four. He peeked around Malcolm to where Patsy hovered like a shadow.

"Your brother is a know-it-all, Patsy," he said.

Her big eyes grew even bigger. "Of course," she said. "He does know everything."

Thomas groaned, and Malcolm punched him lightly on

the shoulder. Caroline motioned for Patsy to come and sit with her. Thomas ambled restlessly up to the courthouse door and tried to peek in through the crack.

"What is taking them so long?"

"What does it matter?" Malcolm said. "They're goin' to find him guilty of forgin' a document, and they'll slap him into the stocks."

Thomas glanced over at the stocks and pillory that loomed like a threat in the courthouse yard. He'd been in the stocks himself once, and he didn't wish that shame on anyone—except perhaps Xavier Wormeley.

"Why did he do such a thing anyway?" Caroline said.

"I asked Master Hutchinson that," Malcolm said. "He says poor Xavier just wants to feel important and have people notice what he's doing."

Thomas swallowed hard. He'd heard Papa say that, too. Each time he did, it gave Thomas a pang of guilt. Hadn't he been trying to do the same thing himself? But he sighed. At least he had God to turn to. It didn't seem that Xavier Wormeley did, for all his prancing into the church every Sunday with his cape sailing out behind him.

The courthouse door opened then, and all four of them jumped. Robert Taylor slipped out into the thin, late-November sunlight and handed a paper to Malcolm. As Malcolm frowned at it, Robert turned to the other children.

"My case came up first. You'll still have to wait for news of Mr. Wormeley."

"What does this mean, sir?" Malcolm asked.

"It means that Patsy's master in Hampton has agreed to sell his rights to her service to anyone in Williamsburg who is willing to pay the price."

"You, Papa?" Caroline's eyes were shining with expectation, but her father shook his head sadly.

"I'm sorry, Caroline," he said. "You know I would take Patsy in if I could, but our position here is so fragile. If we were forced to flee. . . ."

He didn't finish, and Caroline didn't ask him to. His face was working hard to keep back tears.

Caroline turned to Thomas. "What about your papa?" she said.

Thomas shrugged unhappily. The previous night, his father had told him that as much as he would like to bring Patsy into their family, there was simply no more money. He had given much of his fortune for the war, and England was no longer buying crops from Americans.

"But pray, Thomas," he had said. "And God will take this cross from our shoulders, eh?"

Thomas had gone up to his room and prayed for hours. There had been a lot to catch up on with a God he'd forgotten to talk to for so long.

Robert Taylor went off toward his house, and the children sank down on the steps again with their chins in their hands. Patsy looked anxiously at her brother.

"Don't worry," he said to her. "You don't have to go back to Hampton."

She nodded uncertainly, but there was fear in her eyes.

I have to find a place for her! Thomas thought. And then

he stopped himself. *Lord, please help. Please help me carry this cross.*

"Look there!" Malcolm said.

Thomas followed his eyes to a wagon that was making its way slowly from the direction of Jamestown Road.

"Thomas!" Caroline cried from the top step. "They have Walter Clark in there!"

Thomas scrambled to her side and shielded his eyes with his hand. She was right. Red-faced Walter Clark sat in the back, his chapped hands tied in front of him, his head bowed and lolling back and forth with the rocking of the wagon.

"They've found him!" Caroline said. "I suppose they're taking him off to jail."

Malcolm stood up and narrowed his eyes in Walter's direction. "As well they should, after what he did to Thomas."

But the wagon didn't make its way down the Duke of Gloucester Street toward the jail, which was at the end, near Francis's shop. It creaked around the corner at Nassau Street and continued on.

"Where are they going?" Caroline asked.

Malcolm gave Thomas a poke. "It could be hours before Xavier's case is decided. Let's follow that wagon."

So the four of them, with Patsy enthroned safely on her brother's back, ran up Nassau Street in the wake of the wagon. Caroline skipped to keep up with Thomas.

"Aren't you afraid, seeing him so close?" she said. "He was going to kill you!"

Thomas felt his chest, but his heart wasn't hammering. He didn't feel frightened at all. Somehow, he only felt sad.

As he watched, Walter let his rumpled head bob to the side, and their eyes met. There was no light in them to show that he recognized Thomas. He just looked back down at his hands and watched them open and close.

"He didn't really want to kill me," Thomas said. "All he wanted to do was go fight in the war so he would feel important."

"Where are they taking him, Malcolm?" Patsy asked from her brother's back.

Malcolm stopped at the corner of Nassau and Francis Streets, and Caroline and Thomas gathered beside him. It was obvious where they were taking him. Caroline gasped, and Thomas chewed hard at the inside of his mouth.

"What is that place?" Patsy said. "It looks dreadful!"

"It's the Public Hospital for Persons of Insane and Disordered Minds," Malcolm said. He looked at Thomas. "See? I remembered."

"What does that mean?" Patsy asked.

"It means he was crazy to attack Tom like that!" Caroline said fiercely. "That hospital is exactly where that man should be!"

But Thomas didn't agree. *What was it Clayton once said? They are just people who are so unhappy that they've lost their ability to reason like the rest of us.* Maybe there was a way Walter could be happy again. But could it happen in that scary, awful place?

He watched with the others as the man driving the horse

climbed down and joined the other man at the back of the wagon. Together they took Walter by the elbows and guided him down to the ground.

"Here we are, Mr. Clark," said one man. "This is going to be your home for a while."

Walter nodded vaguely.

"We think you'll be quite comfortable here," the other one said. "You just tell us what you need."

Even from where he stood, Thomas saw Walter's eyes come to life.

"I'll need a gun," Walter said. "If I'm to join my company in Carolina, I'll need my weapon."

The men didn't even blink.

"We'll have to see about that," one of them said. "You'll need to rest for a while first. You've had a time of it."

Walter nodded and smiled a vacant smile. "It was quite a battle," he said.

His attendant nodded, too. "I'm sure it was," he said gently.

"Sir! Sir, can you wait a moment?"

Thomas recognized his own voice as he left his friends and ran to the wagon. "May I ask you a question?" he said.

The men nodded, and one of them said, "Certainly."

"Would it be all right if I came to see Mr. Clark here in the hospital?"

The man looked at Walter. "Would you like for this young man to come and visit you while you're here, Mr. Clark?"

For an answer, Walter raised his tied-together hands to

his forehead. "I would salute you, Captain Hutchinson," he said. "But they have me bound. I'm a prisoner of war, you know."

Thomas stared. One of the men winked at him. "You come by anytime, son," he said. "I think it would do Mr. Clark here some good."

Thomas watched until they had disappeared inside the hospital, all the while gently guiding Walter along and talking softly to him. Thomas heard Caroline slip up beside him.

"What will they do to him in there?" she said.

"I think they're going to help him," Thomas said.

The excitement had drained from the morning, and suddenly everything looked as bleak as the naked November trees that had long since dropped all their brilliant leaves.

"That made me sad," Caroline said as they trailed away from the hospital.

"Think how Lydia must feel," Thomas said. "I wonder if she even knows."

Malcolm shifted Patsy on his back and looked at them with his bright, snapping eyes. "Perhaps we should go and tell her. We have no place for our games yet, so that will give this Fearsome Foursome something to do while we're waiting for news of Xavier Wormeley."

Having a purpose brightened everyone's spirits.

"Do you know something?" Caroline said. "Perhaps we don't really need a place. Any place we're all together belongs to us."

"A sound thought, lassie!" Malcolm said, and led the way to Lydia Clark's.

But when they first arrived, Thomas's heart sank. The house looked even more dilapidated than usual, and he was afraid Lydia had left Williamsburg. But when they knocked, she peeked out from behind a dusty curtain and then flung open the door. As Caroline and Malcolm stared in amazement, she held out her arms at once to Patsy, and the little girl climbed down and threw her own thin little limbs around Lydia's waist.

"Glory be!" Malcolm said.

"How did Patsy come to know Lydia?" Caroline said.

But Thomas didn't answer. He had an idea brewing in his head, an idea that Papa should hear about.

He had to wait a while, though, because he had to report to Francis Pickering for work. There was still no word about Xavier, and Caroline promised that she and Patsy would come and tell him as soon as they heard.

When Thomas pushed open the shop door, he froze.

The shelves and cabinets were full again, and old Francis was standing on a chair putting the last of them away.

"Close that door, Hutchinson!" he wheezed from his high perch. "You're letting in all the cold air. We don't have endless firewood, you know!"

Thomas let the door clang behind him, but he continued to gaze at the shelves that were bulging with black bottles and blue-and-white jars. They might as well have been filled with candies, he was so happy to see them.

"What happened?" he said.

"The army has been here," Francis said. "It took a wagon

and three soldiers to bring all of this back." He climbed stiffly from the chair and looked over his spectacles at Thomas.

"If the wounded start coming in," he said, "they will come in and pay me for whatever they need. I'll donate what I can, of course. No one can accuse Francis Pickering of not supporting the revolution!"

"No, sir!" Thomas said quickly.

"But in the meantime, we'll have medicines for our own people." He coughed roughly. "Thanks to you."

His faded eyes shifted, and Thomas realized with a jolt that the old man was embarrassed. Thomas shrugged and looked at the plank floor.

"It's a fact, boy!" Francis said. "I was too proud and stubborn to ask for anyone's help. You weren't—and thank the Lord." He cleared his throat again. "I almost gave up, too, but I'll know better next time. You remind me, boy, eh?"

Thomas shuffled his feet, but he felt his chest swell.

Late that afternoon when he left the shop, Thomas felt like running. It was as if he were so light now that he thought maybe he could fly. He took off up the Duke of Gloucester Street, thinking that he was nearly ready to sprout wings, when he saw Caroline skipping toward him with Patsy, limping, trying to keep up.

As they got closer, Thomas could see that Caroline's dimples were firmly in place, and even Patsy was grinning her crooked-toothed smile.

"They found Xavier guilty?" Thomas cried.

Instead of answering, Caroline grabbed one of Thomas's hands and Patsy the other.

"We have something to show you, Tom," Caroline said, brown eyes sparkling.

"What?"

"You have to wait and see!"

Thomas was so anxious to see that he let them drag him by the hands toward the courthouse. It really wasn't so bad, having girls actually touch him—

But that thought was erased when they reached the square. There, with his floppy jowls and sausage hands sticking out of the stocks, was Xavier Wormeley. His poke-hole eyes had completely disappeared inside his face.

"They found him guilty," Caroline whispered to Thomas. "He's to stay in the stocks until nightfall—and after that, he won't be the magistrate anymore." She clapped her hands. "Isn't it wonderful?"

But as he said good-bye to the girls and headed for home, Thomas didn't feel like celebrating. Walter and Xavier had both gotten what they deserved. Why, he wondered, was that sad somehow?

One thought brightened his spirits, though. Now when he was sad, he had people he could tell . . . and Papa came to mind first. Besides, Thomas had an idea to tell him about.

He was hurrying up the back steps of the Hutchinson house when the back door opened and Esther appeared with a basket full of Mama's clothes. There would be laundry to do tomorrow.

Thomas expected her to shake a finger at him and tell

him to be sure to wipe his feet before he went inside, but instead she set the basket down and rubbed her gnarled old hands together.

"May I have a word with you?" she said.

Thomas stared. She didn't usually ask permission.

"I never want it to be said that Esther McDuff is too proud to admit when she's been wrong," she said. "And I was wrong about you. You were only bearin' your burdens like everyone else when you took to orderin' Malcolm about and such." She tilted up her double chin. "You're every bit as good a young man as he is, Master Thomas."

With that she nodded her head a dozen times, picked up her basket, and waddled off down the steps. All the way to the laundry, she muttered, "Of course you are. I was the one raised you from the cradle to here. . . ."

That, Thomas decided, was worth celebrating. With a grin that stretched from earlobe to earlobe, he hurried to Papa's library and peeked in the door. Papa was sitting at his desk, studying a piece of paper.

"Thomas," he said, "come in. I was about to send for you. I have something to share with you."

"I have something to share with you, too, Papa—when you're finished."

John Hutchinson put the paper down and looked carefully at his son. "No," he said. "You speak first this time. I think you've earned that right."

Thomas tried not to look too pleased with himself as he laid out a plan that had been brewing in his head all day.

"Robert Taylor says Patsy's master in Hampton has

agreed to sell his rights to her services to someone in Williamsburg. I think I've found someone. She's all alone now, and it's said she has money, and she loves Patsy, and Patsy loves her."

"Who is this vision of perfection?" Papa asked.

"Lydia Clark, sir," Thomas replied, and he bumbled on in his excitement. "I know her husband is strange—but he's going to get help—we saw them take him to the Public Hospital, and they were nice to him—he isn't a bad man really—and Lydia—she's just like any of us—"

Papa was holding up his hand, and Thomas stopped and chewed on his mouth.

"You don't have to convince me further, Thomas," his father said. "I'll speak to Lydia Clark this evening—after I meet with George Fenton."

Thomas felt his eyes spring open. "Are you buying a gun, Papa?"

John Hutchinson shook his head. "No. I'm buying back your grandfather's watch."

"Oh" was all Thomas could think of to say.

There was a long, sad silence, until Papa picked up the piece of paper from his desk. "I would like for you to hear this."

"Yes, sir," Thomas said. He sat back in the chair and began to gnaw on his fingernail. The look on his father's face told him it was going to be that kind of news.

Papa read:

Dearest Father,
I cannot tell you where I am, because the position

Alexander has acquired for me requires the utmost secrecy. Just know that I am working for the Patriot cause, just as you are. I hope you will understand that I had choices to make and I had to make them as I saw fit, even though they went against your wishes. Please forgive me. There is little time for me to pray. I hope you will do that for me.

I can tell you this—there is no need to worry about Tarleton's dragoons coming to Williamsburg for the time being. But watch out for Benedict Arnold. He seems bent on copying Tarleton in the Tidewater. I would rather die than see anything happen to any of you.

As for Alexander Taylor, please tell his family that I presume he is safe. He is a smart young man.

> *As ever, your son,*
> *Samuel Hutchinson*

Papa rolled up the paper.

"Not smart enough," he said. "Alexander has still left me in doubt as to where his loyalties actually lie." He shook his head. "Something bothers me about this letter, Thomas. What do you think it is?"

Thomas could think of only one thing. He stopped chewing on his nail and said, "Sam didn't find out whether it was a cross or a burden."

Papa's eyebrows rose, and a small, sad smile creased across his face.

"Which do you think it is?" he asked.

Thomas shrugged. "I don't know, sir. You said we each

have to go to God to find out."

For a moment, all the sadness went out of his father's smile. John Hutchinson stood up and reached for his waist-coat.

"Why don't you come for a walk with me, Thomas?" he said. "I'm going to buy a watch back, and I think I know a Hutchinson who deserves to carry it home."

Thomas stood up, too, and his chest puffed out, and his shoulders squared.

He knew he would carry that watch like a cross.